A R[illegible]

Jessica w[illegible] to the picture of beauty she presented. "See"—she artlessly lifted the hem of her gown well above shapely ankles—"now I even have on proper slippers, so you should have no complaints." She smiled innocently, assuming she had waylaid his concerns.

When Gareth finally managed to speak, he was surprised at the calmness of his voice. "Thank you. Now please lower your skirts! It is not proper to be showing one's limbs to gentlemen!"

Jessica looked up at him as he coldly escorted her downstairs. She couldn't fathom the man's moods at all. "Are you always in such a bad humor, or do you just take exception with me?"

Gareth glowered down at her. "Are you always so impertinent, or simply trying my temper again? I cannot imagine what manner of rackety school the laird sent you to that taught you no more sense of decorum! Did they instruct you in *any* of the refinements of young ladies?"

Otherwise Engaged

Jacquelyn Gillis

J

JOVE BOOKS, NEW YORK

OTHERWISE ENGAGED

A Jove Book / published by arrangement with
the author

PRINTING HISTORY
Jove edition / January 1992

ISBN: 0-515-10732-8

Jove Books are published by The Berkley Publishing Group,
200 Madison Avenue, New York, New York 10016.
The name "JOVE" and the "J" logo
are trademarks belonging to Jove Publications, Inc.

PRINTED IN THE UNITED STATES OF AMERICA

10 9 8 7 6 5 4 3 2 1

Otherwise Engaged

Chapter One

It would have delighted an Irish heart, particularly male, to see Jessica Lynn O'Donovan skipping down the heather-strewn hill. The afternoon sun burnished the red glints of her wind-tousled curls and warmed the gentle sprinkling of freckles on her lightly tanned face.

Unfortunately the male that watched her gracefully leap across the footstones of his creek was neither Irish nor delighted.

Gareth St. John, the most proper Earl of Cantonley, was beyond being pleased by anything other than his own well-ordered London home, at present an impossible distance away. It had been an exceedingly annoying week.

The earl muttered a most ungentlemanly exclamation as the young miss ran right up to the front entrance rather than going to the side servant's door. His mood precluded his being mollified even by the delightful flash of ankle as Jessica lifted her skirts and skipped happily up the steps.

"Barefoot yet!" Gareth sniffed in disdain as he turned

from the upstairs library window with absolutely no intention of answering the expected knock.

The earl was alone at the McDowell manor. He had pensioned off the elderly couple who had tended to the old laird during his last years. The two servants had been packed off the first of the week to a residence nearer their children on the North Sea coast, while the earl remained to inventory the estate before assigning it to a local solicitor for sale.

Gareth frowned yet again on thinking of the inconvenience of managing a perfect stranger's affairs, despite being the stranger's heir. He had not even known of his distant relative Laird Roland McDowell until having been approached by the Irish solicitor bearing the news of the laird's passing.

The earl was shocked from his thoughts by hearing, not the expected knock, but the front door slamming and a lilting voice calling "Papa? I'm home! Marie?"

Papa? The girl must be some kin of the old butler. That certainly gave her no right to be storming into the manor like this! Gareth strode downstairs just in time to see the girl's skirt flit around the corner into the marbled music room. The earl stiffened in utter disbelief as she lightly played a few notes on the pianoforte. That was really outside of enough!

Jessica did a graceful pivot on the smooth marble floor, enjoying the swirling lavender stripes of her cambric gown multiply reflected in the long peer glasses of one of the music room's walls. Flitting by the piano, she experimentally tried a few more notes of a new Chopin she had recently learned. The laird must be in the gardens, she thought. The music room with the current copy of *Rural Repository* or the gardens with their prize rose bushes were usually his favorite places. On an afternoon such as this she should have known to try the gardens first! Jessica danced over to the door, treating herself to one last pirouette on the smooth floor, and crashed headlong into a hard masculine chest.

Gareth let out an expletive he normally would have never thought of using in the presence of even a serving wench as he grasped the girl's slight shoulders to keep the both of them from being upended.

"Sir!" Jessica said, shocked enough to overcome her surprise at running into him. "Papa does not sanction such language!"

This unfortunate observance, needless to say, did nothing to becalm the now livid lord. He was, however, momentarily rendered incapable of a sane reply by the bits of strange debris that had appeared on his most favored Marceilles waistcoat. "What in the name of heaven?" Gareth glared down to find that the girl had been clutching some manner of vegetation which was now crushed all over his chest.

"It is only heather, for goodness sake."

The earl stiffened in disbelief as Jessica quite disrespectfully brushed the offending particles from his person.

"Whoever are you?" she added quarrelsomely, annoyed that he was spoiling her homecoming. Although she had seen the laird only a few weeks ago, it had been a full six months since she'd traveled to the manor.

Jessica didn't wish to waste any more time talking to this pompous man, although he was startlingly handsome she noted, except that he was frowning so.

Lord St. John, generally regarded as the most elegantly restrained of the *ton* Corinthians, found himself with the definite urge to shake the chit. "Perhaps you would be so kind as to enlighten me as to *your* identity and explain what *you* are doing here?" he said, exerting a strong effort to keep a polite tone of voice.

Jessica looked up, momentarily daunted at his tone, but

after a second she raised her chin and attempted a cool authority. After all, who was this man? "I am Jessica Lynn O'Donovan. Lady Jessica," she added for effect, though not too sure of her claim to such a title, "and this, sir, is my home, now that I'm finished school, that is."

As the lord showed no sign of being impressed, Jessica belatedly felt a twinge of concern at finding herself alone with such an unfriendly personage. "Um, where is my grandfather?" She glanced past him, hoping the laird, or at least one of the servants, would have heard the commotion.

Gareth stared at her. "May I be so bold as to ask just who is your grandfather?" He had a sudden feeling he wouldn't find the answer pleasing.

"Laird Roland McDowell, of course." Jessica sniffed. "Do you not even know whose home you are in?"

In his dismay, Gareth overlooked the impertinence. He had been told nothing of any granddaughter. Skeptically he perused the unprepossessing appearance of the girl before him. Lady O'Donovan? This personage a lady? Obviously there was more to this situation than met the eye, Gareth decided, silently cursing the fates for having embroiled him in this wretched dilemma.

Jessica fidgeted in the awkward silence, bringing Gareth's mind back to his duty. Whatever the chit's reason for being here, she obviously hadn't heard of the laird's recent passing.

Gareth frowned at the chore of informing her, but stoically tried to soften the moment. "Let us retire to the parlor. I must speak with you," he said quietly.

Jessica drew back, suddenly frightened by the man's change of mood. "I think not. I prefer to speak to Papa—we have not been properly introduced!"

Gareth shook his head at her sudden recollection of propriety, however the trembling in her voice made him somewhat contrite for his previous brusqueness. She was, after all, little more than a child.

"I am Gareth St. John, Earl of Cantonley, from London. I fear I must serve as the bearer of some unfortunate news. Laird McDowell died—"

"Died?" Jessica interrupted in horror. "No! You are lying!" She tried to duck around the man, but he caught her and held her firmly by the shoulders. "Papa," Jessica cried.

"Child, restrain yourself! Laird McDowell has been buried a fortnight."

"No, it cannot be. It—it must be some mistake." But looking up she saw the truth of his words in his eyes. "What—how did he—?" Her voice broke and she couldn't finish the sentence.

"Apparently, his heart failed. The laird died quite peacefully during his sleep. You must recall he was very old," Gareth counseled her gently. "Being a distant relative, I was summoned as the only kinsman." This fact brought the lord's initial suspicions back to mind. "The authorities mentioned nothing about a granddaughter." He raised a brow questioningly, but Jessica paid him no heed.

"Papa—dead! I cannot believe—he is gone!" Jessica wiped her tears on her sleeve, distractedly, until Gareth felt compelled to sacrifice a fine monogrammed handkerchief.

He studied her cautiously as she struggled for control. It would not be the first time "relatives" had appeared from out of the woodwork for an unallotted estate.

"Come," he said, and finally got her to precede him into the adjoining parlor, then seated her, waiting a moment while she dabbed at her eyes. "You say Laird McDowell was your grandfather? No one has so much as mentioned a granddaughter, not even the laird's servants."

Jessica then remembered the old couple. "Where are Arthur and Marie?"

"They have already been pensioned off," Gareth told her impatiently. "There is no one here but myself. I have been preparing the manor for sale. But back to the question, why is it no one seems to know of your existence?"

For sale! Jessica felt her heart sink at his words. It seemed the fates had intervened against her again. The laird had promised that once she had finished her schooling she could come and live with him. He had said he would acknowledge her as his grandchild, but apparently it wasn't to be. And she had introduced herself so proudly as a "lady" to this nobleman! She sighed and looked up at the earl, finally acknowledging his question.

"No one—is—aware that I am the laird's granddaughter. Papa was going to arrange—"

"No one knows of your relationship?" the earl interrupted with a raised brow. "I'm afraid I find that a bit—odd." Doubtless, it was as he had first suspected—just an awkward attempt to gain from the estate. Suspicions all but confirmed, Gareth determined to find out who had put the girl up to this felonious charade. She didn't seem of enough sophistication to have conceived the plot herself.

Jessica read his censure and lifted her chin proudly. "I know you have no reason to believe me, however it is the truth. Papa paid for my school and clothes, but he—he didn't want anyone to know of our relationship. He promised after I finished school, I should come and—" Jessica's voice broke and she looked down, biting her lip to keep from crying again.

Gareth sniffed. "Why should the laird refuse to acknowledge you if you were his granddaughter?" It was time to put an end to these theatrics. "I think perhaps before you continue I should inform you I am aware the laird had only one child, a son. And that son was engaged to be married when he was killed in a carriage accident," he said coldly. "Further, the woman Robert McDowell was engaged to now lives in London. She married another man and her children all live with her."

"You speak of Lady Westley," the girl surprised him by acknowledging softly. "Papa told me that she was betrothed to his son. I did not intend to suggest—" She hesitated in embarrassment. "The laird's son Robert McDowell *is* my father, but he—didn't—marry my mother," she finally managed.

Gareth frowned. So, she was an illegitimate child, or at least claiming to be one. As such was certainly not uncommon, he had no real reason to discredit it. Nonetheless, there was the matter of her convenient appearance at this very moment, most likely put up to this touching little scene by a mother hopeful of some gain. "Why is your mother not with you?"

"My mother died—giving birth to me." Jessica plucked at her skirt nervously. She knew this lord did not believe she was Robert McDowell's daughter. She stared at the door and wished she could just leave, but suddenly realized now that she had left school, she literally had nowhere to go.

Jessica thought frantically, dashing the fresh tears back in annoyance. The Brantons, who the laird had turned her over to as an infant, had always been kind to her. They lived in the next village. Perhaps she could stay with them until she could find a position of some type. But as neither of the old couple could read or write, she hadn't been in contact with them for several years.

Gareth had been considering her manner of dress. He knew enough of ladies' styles to know that for all her lack of slippers the gown she wore was not something a village maid would normally possess. But then again, the dress easily could have been handed down from the daughter of some local peer or the other. "You say the laird had been supporting you? What is this—school—you've been off attending?"

"The Rougette School for Young Ladies. It is in Perth. You can verify that! Papa *was* paying the sisters, and he sent me an allowance each month."

"Hmm, I see." The earl kept his tone quite casual. "Of course. But I must allow to being curious as to why the laird should suddenly wish to acknowledge you as a McDowell just now, when he had obviously not chosen to do so heretofore?"

Jessica was not fooled by his considering manner. "My lord, I know you do not believe me and I will not be patronized. So, I see no further reason to continue this—interrogation!" Jessica stood to leave.

"Sit down and answer me, girl!" the earl, scarcely accustomed to such disrespect, ordered in a voice even his peers would hesitate to challenge.

Startled, Jessica returned to her seat.

"Well? I asked you a question." Gareth was thoroughly impatient with the whole situation. "Why do you expect me to believe the laird would have suddenly acknowledged you as his granddaughter?"

Jessica forced herself to look at the situation from his point of view. After all, it was an unlikely situation. "Papa was best friends with Lady Westley's father," Jessica explained tentatively. "It seemed they had always wanted their children to marry. Robert and Lord Westley's daughter had become engaged and were to wed in the spring, but then my fa—the laird's son, fell in love with my mother, Mary O'Donovan. He *was* going to marry her, but he was killed before he could."

The earl considered that quite unlikely. But she did seem sincere in at least believing herself this Robert's daughter. Even were it so, the earl wondered at the laird supporting the girl all those years—a simple settlement was generally considered sufficient in such cases. He certainly couldn't believe the man had intended moving the girl in with him and establishing her as his legitimate heir.

"You have as yet presented no reason why the laird would not have acknowledged you to his solicitor at the very least."

"Papa told me he didn't wish to hurt his friendship with Lady Westley's father. He said that he had wanted to wait until some time had passed and Lady Westley was—settled—so it wouldn't cause her and her family embarrassment to learn of me. He even had me use my mother's maiden name—" Jessica hesitated. It sounded like a weak reason even to her, but she had to try to convince him.

"The Lady Westley has been *settled* for some years," the earl observed dryly. "In fact, I am quite familiar with her family. She has children almost of an age with yourself." He tired of playing with the girl and decided to confront her outright. "I don't know who has put you up to this, but obviously they are unaware that even if you are an illegitimate child of Robert McDowell, you would not inherit without a proper will to that effect. Exactly what is it you expect to gain from this?"

The girl looked at him blankly for a moment before understanding sent fury flashing through her jade eyes. "I came here hoping for a grandfather and a home, Your *Lordship*," she spat at him, "not an estate! I realize I have no legal claims, so you need have no fears of having to share your bloody inheritance!"

Gareth was dumbstruck by her temerity in accusing *him*, the Earl of Cantonley, one of the wealthiest noblemen in all of England, of coveting some bucolic Scot's pile of stones! He sputtered in shock as the girl ran from the room.

"Come back here!" he thundered, with no effect on the fleeing girl. Gareth cursed under his breath as he wrestled with the aged wooden door she'd slammed resoundingly behind her. By the time he reached the front entrance, the girl had already leapt the stream. The earl stood watching in exasperation as the lone figure ran back up the hill. Well, she was none of his concern. He turned away. He had been dealt enough problems in settling this accursed estate!

Gareth's thoughts, however, would not let him be. But what if she really was the laird's granddaughter, legitimate or not, and had left school? It was entirely possible that the girl could have nowhere to go. It was feasible that the laird had planned to let her stay with him and labor as a housemaid or some such, which could account for her appearance.

Gareth St. John was a man with a firm sense of responsibility and could not, with a clear conscience, simply forget the girl. No matter what Banbury tale she was trying to cozen him with, she was obviously an innocent and there were too many evils that could befall a child such as she on her own.

Muttering resignedly, the earl stomped out to the kitchen courtyard where he'd secured his mount, and was soon galloping up the hill after the vanished figure.

Jessica was out of breath and sobbing as she sank down on the dressmaker's stoop where the coachman had deposited her traps. On arrival, she had taken the footpath across the field to the manor, planning to have Arthur return with the cart for her belongings. She'd arrived after shop hours and the seamstress and other shopkeepers had already gone. Now it would soon be dark and Jessica hadn't the slightest idea what to do. She didn't really know anyone in this village. The laird had discouraged her associating with people in his own neighborhood the few times she'd been here, not wishing her identity to become known.

The old laird had left Jessica in such straits unwittingly. At first he hadn't cared for the child, though he had promised his son that he would take care of her. On his deathbed, Robert had barely managed to gasp out Mary O'Donovan's name and that she was with child. Though shocked at his studious son's indiscretion, the laird had promised to take care of the girl and their child when it arrived. When this still didn't seem to comfort the dying boy, the laird had reluctantly agreed even to acknowledge the infant as his grandchild and a McDowell when it was born.

The laird had convinced himself it was acceptable to put off the disagreeable task of seeking out the woman until after a period of mourning. When he finally arrived in Ireland, it was only to find she had died in childbirth. The infant, a girl, was discovered in the safekeeping of a neighbor woman. Unable to convince the woman to keep the child, he had resignedly brought Jessica Lynn O'Donovan back with him to Scotland.

It had been easy to excuse the delay in letting anyone know of the child's existence. Surely, there was no cause to add this embarrassment to Lady Westley's grief. It seemed quite sufficient to have the babe cared for and arrange for her schooling when she was of age. In fact, it had only been in recent years that the laird had forced himself to visit Jessica and finally inform her of the kinship. On doing so, he was surprised to find not a bitter reminder of his son's indiscretion, but a delightful, lovely young woman who was a kindred spirit. He cautiously allowed her to stay with him on a few holidays and had determined during the last visit to have her come and live with him after her school was finished that term. The laird had thoroughly intended notifying his solicitor of their relationship and having him prepare a codicil to his will. Unfortunately, that arduous task had been put off too long.

Jessica could think of nothing to do but try to find someone in the village who would take her on to Kilhaven where the Brantons lived. She had a small amount of the pocket money the laird had given her in her last allowance. Bleakly, Jessica now understood why they hadn't received word from the laird before school was out as expected. But no one had been unduly concerned as the school had been released a week early that year. The Rougette sisters had been leaving on one of their summer sojourns; in fact, their ship had been sailing that very day. Jessica had convinced them it was all right for her to take the mail-coach home. As one of the other girls and her maid accompanied her, their own destination being even further south, it had seemed quite safe. Of course, no one could have foreseen any of this.

Jessica was rather forlornly counting the few shillings she had remaining in her reticule when the earl pulled up his bay before her.

The unwelcome twinge of conscience on seeing the girl's pitiful plight only caused the earl further annoyance. "I told you to come back!"

Jessica looked up sullenly. "I see no reason I should obey some stranger's orders!"

"I am the Earl of Cantonley, girl," he shouted, "and on the outside chance that you are in fact related to the laird, I am your eldest male relative." He almost choked on the thought.

Jessica merely gave him a disdainful glance. "I don't suppose you would know what it would be for post fare to Kilhaven?"

Gareth leapt from his horse. "Kilhaven! Kilhaven be damned! You are coming with me!" He practically snatched her up by the arm. "And you *will* begin showing some respect!"

Jessica cringed back from him in terror. She had never been around many males, and certainly none such as this very large, furious, *cursing* man! "Your Lordship, please! You are hurting me."

Gareth realized what he was doing and released her, disgusted with himself. What in the blue blazes was it about this headstrong chit that served to provoke him so completely? It must just be the whole blamed situation! Gareth tried desperately to regain his decorum, but couldn't quite bring himself to apologize. "You had best learn not to try my temper!" he finally managed. "Now what is in this—Kilhaven?"

A very subdued Jessica hesitantly explained that the Brantons lived there. "They are the couple who raised me until I went off to school at eight years of age. I'm sure they would not mind my boarding with them again until I can find a position—"

"A position?"

"Yes, my lord. Perhaps I can find someone who needs a governess or—"

"Governess!" Gareth again cut her off. "You are a child yourself," he scoffed.

"I am seventeen years," Jessica offered carefully, fearing his renewed anger. "I should be deemed qualified to teach young children."

In surprise, the earl studied her carefully for the first time. He realized he had assumed she was younger from the cut of her dress, and the way her hair fell down her back all atumble. He frowned thoughtfully—the solicitor had said the son was killed about seventeen years before.

The lord glanced over at her traps stacked neatly on the porch. The number of them and grade of leather supported her story of a better girls' school. In a quandary, he pondered for another moment before forcing himself to a decision. "I am staying at the village inn tonight. I shall bespeak a room for you as well, and tomorrow we shall seek out this couple who raised you." He realized he owed that much to any young girl in distress, and it wasn't really far to the next village. "Now come along. I'll send someone back for your effects." Then remembering, he glanced in disdain at her bare feet, and said, "You do have slippers?"

The lord watched impatiently as Jessica slipped her stockings and shoes from behind the trunks where she had left them. He looked away, shaking his head in wonderment, as she casually brushed the soil from her feet with her hands before donning her shoes. He hoped he could pawn off this little hoyden on the old couple before anyone he knew found him escorting her. The Earl of Cantonley getting caught by a milk-faced schoolgirl! He shuddered. If necessary, he would even pay this couple to take her off his hands, the lord decided with equanimity.

The gentleman in him could not allow the girl to walk the length of the village to its lone inn while he rode, and he certainly didn't intend walking that dusty road in his new Hessians, so rather begrudgingly, Gareth lifted her up before him on his mount.

Jessica, now that the lord wasn't acting quite so fierce, not to mention being quite thoroughly exhausted from both the emotions and exertion, relaxed artlessly against his hard chest. As they rode, Jessica had to acknowledge to herself that she would have been in a most awkward state of affairs without this earl's timely intervention. After considering the matter for a few moments, she finally brought herself to glance up a bit shyly and meet his eyes. "I do appreciate your assistance, sir, and would like to apologize for my previous manners."

Gareth looked at her suspiciously. Not trusting what he considered an intentionally beguiling change of mood, he merely nodded without comment.

Actually, the earl found himself vaguely disconcerted by the soft, now obviously mature, female form relaxed so naturally against his chest. He was considerably relieved when they reached the inn and he could set her down.

Chapter Two

Gareth flipped a half crown to the gaping stable boy with instructions to retrieve the girl's valises. He then escorted Jessica into the large tap room. The inn's proprietor appeared with commendable promptness, bowing effusively to hide his covert glances at the girl with whom the nobleman had returned. "Milord's pleasure?" he asked.

"It has become necessary that I remain for yet another night," Gareth said curtly. "The young lady is my—ward," he said by way of explaining her, "and will be needing a room as well. Her abigail is not along, so perhaps you could be so good as to have a chambermaid attend her."

"Of course, milord." He blandly nodded to Jessica as he bowed. "Milady, I shall send someone to you immediately."

The innkeeper gave a calculating glance back at the two of them as he left. He wouldn't have took a high stickler like that to have fetched him up some local girl. Awful young 'un, too! Ward, indeed! Didn't really matter to him, always glad to have the gentry under his roof as the inn's fees naturally always went up with the guest's titles.

Gareth rankled at the landlord's speculative look, knowing full well what the man was thinking. He looked critically at Jessica, and it was understandable how that bounder dared assume such a thing about him! The girl looked like she might have just come from some roll in the hay, or heather more like. Her hair all atumble, and not a proper color at all! Like ginger or something. And freckles across her nose, of all things! He had never known a genteel woman to allow herself to get freckles. Although, he mused looking closer, somehow the freckles weren't exactly unattractive. In fact, Gareth considered, they vaguely reminded him of his favorite of the pups from that new litter—creamy with reddish brown specks.

"You're glaring at me again!" Jessica, true to her nature, had quickly recovered her spirits.

"I will have you know I do not glare!" The lord glared, angry at being so boldly interrupted from his thoughts.

"If you wish to change your mind about assisting me, I shall be glad to—" Jessica began, but just then the promised chambermaid appeared.

"Milord," she said, and bobbed nervously, unsure whether she should have interrupted an argument between the quality. "Mister Crashen said I was to tend the young miss."

"Yes." Gareth gave Jessica a quelling look that dared her to speak again. "You shall take Miss O'Donovan to her chambers, arrange for her bath, and—do something with her hair!"

He turned to Jessica. "I shall bespeak a private parlor for supper in two hours." With a curt nod, the earl headed to a table in the common room. After this day, he was even willing to risk the contents of the dubious cellar of the village landlord, feeling sorely in need of spirits.

"Milady?" The girl gestured for Jessica to follow her.

Jessica demurely accompanied the chambermaid until out of hearing of the lord, then smiled at the girl. "I am Jessica—you can call me Jess. What is your name?"

The shy maid was flabbergasted at first, but soon with Jessica's natural friendliness, the two girls were confiding happily with each other.

Later, his humor somewhat improved by a surprisingly good port, Gareth repaired to his own chambers to dress for dinner. Lord St. John had refrained from bringing his own rather fastidious valet into the area with him. He feared the man would resign from his service if forced to go into what he too considered barbarous regions, and it was altogether much too difficult to replace a good gentleman's gentleman.

At first on hearing the girlish chatter and giggles coming from the next room as he dressed, Gareth assumed it came from some traveler's daughters. But then he recognized Jessica's voice. That fool innkeeper had given her the adjoining room, doubtless assuming it was his wish! It could only be the chambermaid with which the girl was waxing so familiar. Did she have no sense of propriety at all? Well-schooled young ladies did not fraternize with servants!

He stalked over and rapped loudly on the connecting door. The voices instantly quieted, and after a moment the chambermaid opened the door a crack. "Yes, milord?"

Gareth gave her a cutting look. "It would appear as though you are occupied more in gossiping than in attiring my ward for dinner!"

The young girl cringed away. "I am so sorry, milord. I ain't meant to—"

"Oh don't be so cow-hearted, Katy." Jessica intervened impatiently from behind her. "You have nothing to apologize for. Lord St. John, I initiated the conversation and was enjoying Katy's company. As you can see it has not deterred me in the slightest from my preparations."

Gareth stopped midway to a very biting retort as she came into view. He scarcely believed it was the same girl. She wore a pale green silk round dress, which, though still of a youthful cut, revealed startlingly creamy shoulders and a graceful neck. The girl's mass of brilliant hair hadn't exactly been subdued, if such were even possible, but had been drawn up high with ribbons to fall back in a profusion of curls. Her figure curved sweetly from a high, firm breast down to a naturally delicate waist.

Jessica was oblivious to the picture she presented. "See"—she artlessly lifted the embroidered hem of her gown well above shapely ankles—"now I even have on proper slippers, so you should have no complaints." She smiled innocently, assuming she had waylaid his concerns.

Gareth found himself wondering if perhaps the landlord could have put something in his port! When he finally managed to speak, he was surprised at the calmness of his voice. "Thank you. Now please, lower your skirts." He looked away from the delectable display of leg, and marshaling his thoughts added, a bit belatedly, "It is not proper to be showing one's limbs to gentlemen!"

The earl curtly dismissed the maid. "Tell the innkeeper we shall repair to the parlor to be served."

Jessica looked up at him as he coldly escorted her downstairs. She couldn't fathom the man's moods at all. "Are you always in such a bad humor, or do you just take exception with me?" she finally asked.

Gareth glowered down at her. "Are you always so impertinent, or simply trying my temper again?" he countered, ushering her into the parlor. "I cannot imagine what manner of rackety school the laird sent you to that taught you no more sense of decorum!"

"The Mistresses Rougette have an excellent school!"

Jessica hotly defended the sisters she had come to adore. "It is owned by two highly intelligent ladies. Miss Elizabeth is an excellent artist, and Miss Sophia writes those marvelously droll political satires under the name—oh, but I promised to never reveal her pen name!"

"An artist and satirist manage the school? Marvelous," he snapped sarcastically. "Did they instruct you in *any* of the refinements of young ladies?"

"I have no notion what *you* may mean by 'refinements.' " Jessica raised her chin proudly. "I learned Latin, Greek and French. Italian, I can read but not speak well as yet," she admitted, forgetting her antagonism as she warmed to her subject. "I've finished a number of Greek classics in the original language—those which we had available. I especially adore the originals, don't you? We also learned animal sciences, and I am fascinated with that new work in medicine by—"

Gareth stared at her. He himself knew no Italian at all and had never become very good with Greek. He hadn't even heard of the medical developments she was chattering on about, though had she been a gentleman friend, he would have been delighted to quiz her on them. These were certainly not proper subjects for a lady! This "school" doubtless was one of those talked-of "Dissenters' Academies."

The lord decided to overlook the odd academics, in part because he was somewhat reluctant to elaborate on the matter least she pursue the Greek question. "By female refinements, I was speaking of the cultural aspects proper for young ladies. Music, embroidery, voice, the management of a home—"

"Oh yes, of course we learned those, too." Jessica lightly dismissed his concerns. "I especially love the pianoforte. Miss Elizabeth often fussed because I spent more time playing than on my studies. As to singing, Miss Sophia said my voice is pleasant but too light to carry, so I suppose I could never manage to go on stage." She sighed a bit poignantly, not hearing his muttered, "Thank God!"

"I really haven't the patience for embroidery, but I adore drawing and watercolors. Miss Elizabeth even admitted to being envious of how anatomically correct my animals are."

Gareth drew a breath and opened his mouth, but wisely decided it safer to simply let that subject pass.

"And as for the management of a home," she continued happily. "I can't see what there is to learn. Naturally I can keep correct accounts. I helped with the school's books since neither of the Rougette sisters were fond of figures. The rest, it seems, would just be common sense."

Lord St. John sat silently in consideration. In all his twenty-eight years he'd never come upon such a female as this one! Could it be possible this farce was merely something set upon him by his friends? It seemed like some tomfoolery that devil Lyle might concoct, but then again, he would be too lazy to have come clear to Scotland for a mere ploy, regardless of how elaborate.

Jessica fidgeted during the earl's silence. "I'm, uh, certain the ladies of your acquaintance are much better schooled. Compared to the Highlands, England is such an advanced country, is it not?"

Gareth decided it was time to change the subject and questioned her on her association with the laird.

Jessica explained how that gentleman had not visited her until she was fifteen. "I think he came primarily from a sense of guilt at first. He had promised his son he would acknowledge me, but apparently could not bring himself to tell me I was his grandchild until two years ago. I do wish he hadn't died before I could have really gotten to know him better," she added pensively.

Gareth could think of no comment to that. "Was the laird

the only man at the manor other than the servant when you visited?" He was wondering if perhaps McDowell might have confided her origin, or his intentions to some of his friends.

"Men? No, there was never anyone there, except of course Arthur and Marie."

"Perhaps the laird listed himself as a relative with the school?" he asked hopefully.

"No." Jessica looked down. "He told the sisters I was his ward."

Gareth frowned; it was really difficult to believe her story. Surely, if true, the laird would have left some instructions. He began to realize the girl had probably not been around many men, which, he allowed, perhaps explained her inappropriate attitude toward him. He shuddered to think how she would appear to a proper society like the London *ton*.

The earl had another thought. "This school, you seem to have gotten on well there, perhaps you would wish to return and teach or something?"

Jessica realized he was merely trying to find some way of ridding himself of her as quickly as possible. "The Rougette sisters always leave on tour immediately after the session is over. That is why we were released early this summer. Their ship departed today, in fact. And the school is quite small—there were only five students this year. They would scarcely need another teacher." She looked blindly at her plate for a moment. "My lord, I understand I am an—inconvenience—to you, but truly if you will take me to Kilhaven tomorrow, you needn't concern yourself further on my behalf."

Gareth found himself a bit chagrined at her ease in guessing his thoughts. But her offer might just be a ruse to engage his sympathies and gain the inheritance. Actually after death taxes the estate would not yield enough to support itself. The manor would have to be sold. The money was of no matter to him, and should she really be the laird's relative, he would not object to her receiving it. Except for the management of the principal, Gareth added to himself. Heaven forbid that he might truly find himself shackled with her as a ward! He supposed a solicitor could handle the funds. If she had somewhere to live there should be enough to provide her with sufficient dowry to attract some young man.

Jessica finished her meal halfheartedly. The earl had made no effort to repute the fact that she was an "inconvenience." Somehow it hurt that he hadn't even denied it out of politeness. He really was a relative, at least of sorts, and apparently the only one she might ever know. It would be nice if he liked her, even a little.

The earl appeared sunk in reverie as he sipped his port, and Jessica covertly considered him. He was extremely handsome, though a bit hard looking.

"Sculptured," is how Miss Elizabeth would have defined his features. In fact, thinking of sculptures, the earl reminded Jessica of the bust of a Roman soldier Miss Elizabeth had worked in clay.

Jessica had been fascinated on seeing the figure. In new enthusiasm for that medium, she had borrowed some of Elizabeth's clay to mold her favorite animal figures. After a few tries, however, she had ended up tossing them aside in frustration. "I'm going back to pen and paper," Jessica had grumbled to Elizabeth. "It's easier to draw all that hair on animals than try to mold it. That's probably why you're sculpting a man—they don't have hair all over!" she had joked when her teacher protested that she was giving up too easily.

"No, it is quite simple really. Watch this," Elizabeth had told her, and began defining curled hairs across the bare chest of the sculpture with a pointed tool. "It is much like using a pen."

Jessica had laughed. "Well, perhaps I'll try again, but you must stop. You are ruining your work! People don't really have hair on their chests!"

Elizabeth had merely smiled. "Girls don't, my dear, but men often do."

Remembering, Jessica gave Gareth's chest a speculative look.

Gareth looked down. "Is there perhaps something wrong with my cravat?"

"Hmm?" Jess glanced up questioningly, having been lost in her thoughts.

"My cravat. You are staring quite pointedly at my cravat!"

"Oh, was I? Actually, I was just wondering whether you have hair on your chest."

Lord St. John almost dropped his port. "Jessica!" He was shocked into using the familiar address. "Young women do not ask gentlemen such personal questions!"

"I didn't ask!" she retorted in annoyance. The man was always so blamed touchy. "I merely said I was wondering."

"Properly brought up young ladies do not even wonder about such things," he said cuttingly.

"Oh, fustian! Of course they do. They simply don't admit it. Did you not wonder about girls when you were a boy?"

Gareth had, naturally, but had no intention of admitting so. "Miss O'Donovan!" he growled warningly.

"Oh, for goodness sake, don't get all in a tither again! I apologize if the subject embarrasses you but"—seeing the look in his eyes, she decided perhaps she should mollify him a bit—"how am I supposed to know what proper young ladies should discuss with gentlemen, having scarcely spoken to one, except Papa? If it concerns you so, why don't you just tell me what we may 'properly' discuss?"

Gareth was taken aback by her forthrightness. He had never before encountered anyone remotely like her. Even his *femmes d'armour* would never have dared to speak to him as openly as she! But then, in all honesty, he recognized that the girl really did not know any better. He took a deep breath. "Very well. As you obviously could use the tutelage, I shall attempt to explain." He mulled over the problem a moment and then decided to use his betrothed as an example. "Meredith—that is, most ladies of my acquaintance—discuss, well, whatever are the latest *on dits*—"

"*On dits*? Did you say '*dits*'?" Jessica gave him a puzzled look.

He blinked. "Yes, er, the happenings of society, soirees, musicales, what various personages are doing."

"Oh." She looked rather unimpressed. "I fear I would know little about those. What else should I discuss?"

"Hmm. Well, ladies generally seem to enjoy discussions concerning their new apparel, bonnets and—and the like. Styles. The best modistes—milliners—"

"With you?" she cut in incredulously.

"What?"

"Do they talk about hair styles and bonnets to you? I should think a man would find such talk quite boring."

He did find it unbearably boring. "Those are proper subjects," he told her nonetheless.

Jessica shook her head in wonder. "But surely— Are you married?"

Gareth frowned sternly at her presumption, but as feared, his censure was lost on her. She merely waited for his answer. He finally give up and answered curtly. "No. I shall soon announce my wedding date, however."

"Then I should think you would spend considerable time with your fiancée. The two of you should know each other enough to discuss real things."

"Real things?"

"Yes." Jessica leaned forward eagerly. "What are your interests? What books do you read? What are your thoughts on religion, politics, raising your children—"

"Delicate, unwed ladies certainly do not discuss having children!" the earl corrected with asperity.

Jessica sighed. "Oh, very well. Surely you and your lady discuss books?"

"Miss Meredith does not fritter her time away reading novels such as those 'penny dreadfuls,' if that's what you suggest."

Jessica bridled. "Novels are very interesting and rather enlightening on human behavior. But there are other things to read: journals, newspapers—"

"Young ladies are not expected to bother themselves with the subjects of such writings. Those are for men."

"Oh—" Jessica stopped before saying a word she knew she'd get called down on. "Well, if your fiancée cannot be bothered with anything of substance and hasn't time to read for pleasure, what does she do with her days?"

"Meredith is one of the belles of the season," the earl pointed out haughtily. "She has a very demanding social life. There are the constant balls, soirees, and the like. She has time for little else."

Jessica considered his statement with a frown. "All those parties would be enjoyable on occasion, but it scarcely seems like what one should wish to do constantly."

Gareth privately agreed. Since he had made the decision to wed Meredith, he had become quite weary of the social whirl and looked forward to settling on his country estate. Meredith probably wouldn't stand for it without a fuss though, except when she was with child and had to retire. He sighed at the thought.

"What else do you discuss with your fiancée, my lord?" Jessica probed when he remained silent.

Lord St. John realized that he had never really discussed anything of consequence with Meredith. It was an annoying thought. "I have already told you the proper areas of discussion."

Jessica grimaced. "To be proper then, I should only be discussing my gown with you, for instance?"

Gareth gave a cautious nod. "Yes, that would be acceptable."

"Hmm. Whatever can one discuss about a gown? Although this is one of my favorites." She brightened. "Do you like it? Miss Sophia brought it to me from France. It is made of real silk!" she said, admiring the material of her flowing sleeve.

"The gown is very becoming," the earl allowed, relieved finally to have her assuming a role with which he was familiar.

"Sophia told me some type of worm makes silk, but I can scarcely credit it, though I had no wish to tell her so!" She fingered the soft material. "How could worms make such lovely fabric?"

Gareth smiled, forgetting himself. "Your Miss Sophia was correct. But the worms do not actually make the fabric. They do spin the tiny threads of silk from which it is woven."

"Spin? Like a spider web?" Jessica asked in amazement.

"The silkworm's web is similar, but much, much stronger. Silk was originally from the Far East; China, in fact. The silkworms live there in mulberry trees. They form their cocoons from the silkweb."

Jessica was fascinated and eagerly entreated him to tell her all stages from the silkworm to the finished material. On completion of the lesson, he found himself naturally enlarging upon the story by telling her of his journey to the Orient several years back.

When the innkeeper came to ask if they wished anything more, Gareth was surprised to find it was quite late.

Jessica, too, was amazed how the hours had flown. "I must beg your pardon, my lord. I find I was quite wrong to complain about your suggested subjects of discussion, but I never would have imagined discussing apparel could be so very interesting!"

Who indeed? Gareth thought in bemusement, though it was scarcely like any other discussion he had endured on lady's apparel.

Later, as Lord St. John prepared to retire, he found himself more in charity with the unpredictable lass. He acknowledged to himself with no little surprise that hc had actually enjoyed a rather pleasant evening.

Jessica joined the earl in the parlor for breakfast the following morning. Once again she appeared much the school girl, dressed in a high-necked sprigged muslin dress of pale peach covered by a darker pelisse of twilled sarcenet with only the simplest of narrow work on the hem.

The earl noted her attire with approval, especially the fact that she had somehow managed to restrain the masses of disconcerting hair beneath a prim straw bonnet. Despite her improvements however, he was ready to be finished of the whole affair.

It was still early when the lord's coachman advised the earl that he had Jessica's traps loaded upon the traveling coach ready for departure to Kilhaven. Gareth pulled his watch from its vest pocket and studied it in satisfaction. He could drop the chit off with this Branton couple and be well on his way home to London before noon.

As they exited the inn, Jessica noticed the earl consult his watch and said, "I have not overly delayed your journey."

Gareth ignored a slight sense of guilt; the girl was trying very hard to please him, but certainly he was obliged to do no more than deliver her safely to someone's keeping.

"It is time to depart," he announced firmly, and called for his mount. He decided it wiser to ride beside the coach. It would, after all, be unseemly to encourage the girl to assume a relationship between them.

Jessica said nothing as the coachman handed her into the earl's equipage, but she was disappointed, having enjoyed their conversation of the previous night and hoping it suggested a continuing friendliness on his part. However, it seemed the morning set him, once again, to being the stiff aristocrat.

When they arrived at the village of Kilhaven, Gareth drew his mount alongside the carriage to ask Jessica directions to the Brantons' cottage.

Jessica directed the coach through the village to a narrow path that led to her childhood home, but on arriving was perplexed to find a number of staring children around the well-remembered yard.

"Are you quite certain this is the cottage?" Gareth was again plagued by an uneasy foreboding. "You said an elderly couple lived here?"

"Of course, I lived here for some eight years." Jessica, unasked, let herself out of the carriage and headed to the cottage, forcing Gareth to practically leap from his mount to catch up with her.

They were met at the door by a young matron, who wiped her hands nervously on her apron as she bobbed a curtsy. "May I be of some help, milord?" She waved back the curious urchins.

Lord St. John stepped forward and introduced himself, ignoring Jessica. "We are looking for the Brantons, an older couple who lived here."

"Mercy, milord, Mrs. Branton moved off somewhere in the North Umberlands, to live with her sister, I think she said, when we came here," the woman answered in surprise. "That was over two years ago. Her husband had passed, God rest his soul, some months before, and she didn't care to stay on here alone."

"Where did—"

"Oh, no! Mr. Branton died?" Jessica interrupted Gareth in her concern. She had truly loved the couple. It seemed the few people she'd ever known and cared for had either moved away or died. "Perhaps you would know Mrs. Branton's address?" she asked the housewife.

The matron glanced at the lord in concern. "No milady, I'm sorry." The woman shook her head sympathetically. "The Brantons were some friends of yours, miss?"

"They—they raised me. I had hoped to come stay with them again for a while." Jessica blinked back tears.

The woman gaped in amazement. This fine lady was to stay in this little cottage with a poor old couple! What was the world coming to?

Gareth began to feel a minor panic on seeing the woman's look. "I think perhaps we should—"

But Jessica interrupted again. "The rector, would it still be Jeremy Glover, perchance?" She tried to think of someone else in the village she knew.

"Why yes, miss, but . . ."

Jessica turned to Gareth, who by now was glowering in annoyance. "I'm sure the rector will let me stay at the parsonage until I find somewhere else to live, perhaps—"

"Jessica, I—" This time the earl was totally confounded to find himself being interrupted by the housewife.

"You have nowhere to live, miss?" The woman couldn't contain her astonishment any longer, giving a hard look at the gentleman with the girl. Poor child was probably some light o-love he was tired of, and was now trying to pass off.

Gareth drew himself up stiffly at the woman's look. Good Lord, this stupid girl had gotten him into an even more embarrassing predicament now! "Miss O'Donovan—" he growled warningly.

Typically she misunderstood his concern and rushed on. "You mustn't worry, my lord, the rector has known me since I was a child. He can probably recommend me for some position, too."

The housewife shook her head in disbelief. Pointedly ignoring Lord St. John, she gently said, "Begging your pardon, miss, I know it ain't my place to be making suggestions, but the Reverend Glover is in poor health just now, his gout, with all this damp weather, and the Jensons, their cottage was burned out a month ago, it'll be autumn before it can be rethatched. He's letting them stay in the parsonage. There is a cottage empty in the village, perhaps your—gentleman—could rent it for you."

The earl glanced down at the woman. "Miss O'Donovan is my *ward*, madam! Come, Jessica!" He took her arm, completely mortified. Nothing like this had ever happened to him. That woman obviously thought that he, the Earl of Cantonley, was trying to pawn off some lightskirt on the parish priest!

"But, my lord—" Jessica hung back, understanding neither the woman's assumption nor Gareth's obvious horror.

"Now, I said!" He fairly dragged her into the coach, this time joining her inside in a cold fury.

Jessica looked at him in exasperation. "You've directed the coach the wrong way. The parish house is the other—"

"Quiet, girl!"

Jessica shrank back as he practically yelled at her. "I thought nobles were supposed to be gentlemen!" Jessica pouted, rather unwisely, furthering the earl's feeling that he had again been driven into acting beneath his station. There was something about this female that brought out the worst in him! However, rather than calming his humor, this thought had the opposite effect. He felt like giving the brat a good shaking. Gareth forced himself to remain calm as the coachman maneuvered the carriage back down the narrow lane.

Jessica finally realized that his lordship was thoroughly furious with her again. She didn't understand why, but nonetheless decided it would be prudent to proceed gingerly. "Sir, if you please, I did know several other families here in Killhaven. I'm sure I could—"

Gareth, not about to be subjected to the possibility of such embarrassment again, made a begrudging decision. "You are returning to London with me," he cut her off coldly.

"To London—with you?" Jessica looked at him in amazement.

"I have a widowed aunt who lives with me and manages my home. I daresay she will provide you adequate chaperonage, if that is your concern."

Jessica had no notion of the impropriety of being alone with a man in his home. "No, my lord, I appreciate your offer," she said, confused all the more by the apparent kindness of the offer and the cold manner in which it was made. "It was only that I am surprised. I must admit I had the impression you wished me off of your hands."

"It appears you have become my responsibility!" Gareth snapped, not even bothering to deny her allegation.

Jessica sat in stunned silence for a moment before her Irish temper flared. "I beg your pardon, my lord, but I do not care to be your 'responsibility' or any bloody thing else!" she flung back at him. "Just return to your stupid stuffy London and forget you ever met me!" She leaned out the window. "Driver, stop this carriage immediately!"

The driver pulled up his horses in consternation, just as they re-entered the little village.

"What in heaven's name do you think you are doing?" Gareth grabbed Jessica about the waist as she wrenched the door open before the carriage had even completely stopped.

His quick move left her legs dangling awkwardly outside the carriage.

"I am getting out! And I can manage quite well on my own, Your Lordship. I certainly don't care to be a—a burden to some ill-mannered count!" she shrieked, spinning about to kick futilely at him.

"Earl!" Gareth yelled back, yanking her bodily back into the carriage and then groaning as he looked up and saw the gawking crowd of villagers beginning to gather.

"Earl—duke—count—whatever! I'll not go with you anywhere." Jessica managed to pull away again and leapt from the carriage. "Driver, please hand down my cases."

Amos, the earl's coachman, had never seen the likes of this. Hesitantly he started to reach for the girl's traps, but stopped in amazement as his master stormed from the coach and very unceremoniously scooped the young miss up and flung her back into the carriage. At the earl's angry "Drive on," Amos wasn't about to tarry. He whipped up the horses, glad himself to be away from the astonished villagers. The master had really found him a handful in this miss, though. Amos grinned, hearing some very unladylike exclamations coming from the carriage before the girl was abruptly quieted by the earl's angry roar.

Lord St. John, Earl of Cantonley, leaned back against the finely tooled leather of his carriage to ease the pounding in his head. Never had he had an experience such as that! The blasted chit was likely to be the death of him! He had never been so mortified in all his life! The Earl of Cantonley was renowned throughout London as a stickler for propriety. Heaven forbid his friends should ever get wind of this day! Reluctantly he glanced over to the corner where Jessica was huddled, sniffling miserably, and once again began to feel the brute.

In all fairness, as she had unfortunately reminded him, he had been perfectly willing to abandon her with the Brantons. How had he gotten into this ridiculous mess? That bloody laird's estate . . . heathenish Scots, anyway . . . anyone that could come up with those wailing bags.

Gareth pondered his situation for a moment. At this stage he didn't even care if she was really the laird's granddaughter or not; she could have the blooming estate, all of it! He'd sell the manor and—no, he couldn't wait for that. He'd settle a dowry on the chit himself, soon as he got her to London. Turn her over to Aunt Elizabeth. Aunt Bet would delight in a chance to get out and go to more parties. She was a bit of a rattle herself, so she and the girl should get along fine. She could take her to some minor social events—surely some lad would be interested, with enough dowry . . . Gareth looked over at Jessica speculatively. She really wasn't unsightly, even with the freckles. He frowned as his mind, unbidden, brought up the vision of her in the green silk.

Jessica sensed his attention and gave him a frightened glance. Her eyes were even more emerald now that they were brimming with tears. Gareth sighed and pulled out a fresh handkerchief. "Here, quit being such a blamed watering pot," he said gruffly, and handed her the bit of linen, making a mental note to order a dozen more when he got home—or two dozen at this rate!

The girl accepted the handkerchief in silence and turned back to the window. Gareth considered her a moment, wondering vaguely how long it would take to get her married off. He frowned. She looked too young—scarcely seemed of age to be out of school. No wonder that housewife had glared at him, thinking he was taking advantage of such a child! Gareth drew his mind from that painful scene and returned to his appraisal of the girl.

If she just looked more—English. Her hair was definitely different in color from most of the young ladies making their come out. The color wasn't necessarily bad though, he mused; it was somewhat like that of a good port held up to a candle flame, and the curls almost seemed alive, bouncing about with her every movement where they had loosened themselves from the bonnet's constraint. Gareth's eyes traveled downward in their survey before he forced himself to look away, reminding himself that she was but a child, although his own Meredith was not quite a year older than Jessica.

By the time they stopped at the Red Coach Inn to change horses and partake of tea, Jessica was back in charity with the world in general, if not with Gareth in particular, having decided his temperament was too unpredictable for her tastes.

When they were served their meal, Jessica could no longer restrain her curiosity and decided to risk speaking to him again. "Sir," she began rather hesitantly, "you have not told me what you intend for me when we reach your London home. Do you perhaps have friends that might need a governess or children's maid?"

Gareth looked at her in surprise for a moment before realizing he had in fact told her nothing other than he was taking her to his house. "It will not be necessary for you to seek employment. The laird's estate can support you and supply a dowry." He recognized the inadvisability of letting her know he was advancing the money. "You are of marriageable age. I shall have my Aunt Bet, that is, Lady Elizabeth Trenton, escort you to the usual events for young women. I'm sure you shall not lack for suitors from whom to choose a husband."

Jessica glanced at him, not certain if he had intended the compliment, but decided to give him the benefit of doubt. "Thank you, but I don't understand why you are doing this. I received the impression you were not convinced I am really the laird's granddaughter, and even so, as you mentioned, I have no legal claims."

"On further consideration of the matter, I have decided

appearances indicate you to be as you say, and regardless of the legal necessity, I prefer to follow what I can only presume to be the laird's last wishes."

Jessica considered that in silence for a few moments as they ate. Having become more cautious in her conversations with him, she doubted the wisdom of questioning his change of mind. Of course, she had hoped to marry eventually, but it was not a prospect she would have considered imminent. Jessica gave the earl a rather critical look. If all men were like him, marriage was definitely not something she intended rushing into. As the earl raised his eyebrows inquiringly on catching her look, Jessica decided to skip that thought, merely adding, "I am not sure I would know how to fit into English society."

Doubtless not, Gareth thought to himself, but politely alleviated her concern. "Aunt Bet will be pleased to direct you in whatever is required. I'm sure you shall learn quickly." Or hope so, he added silently, wondering how long he could bear having her in his household. Perhaps he could return to the country while she—but no, it was the height of the season. Meredith would be incensed if he left her for any period of time. Gareth sighed in frustration at this untoward infringement on his orderly lifestyle.

When they finally arrived in London, the weather was quite bleak with a steady drizzle. The rain had been with them since morning, forcing Gareth to share the carriage with the girl, who had become thoroughly restless from being cooped up on the long journey.

After Jessica asked how much further it was for the fifth time, Gareth, also irritable, had thundered that they would be there when they arrived and she was *not* to ask again! At that, Jessica fell into a sulking silence, convinced that not only should she never marry but that she didn't even like men.

But now Jessica, having never been in a city of any size,

could not restrain her enthusiasm on viewing the busy streets crowded with carriages and ware-hawkers out even in the rain. She longed to ask about some of the sights but dared not test the earl's mood again.

They finally entered a less congested area of large, distinguished brownstones. The carriage drew to a halt before one of the more impressive specimens. There followed a flurry of activity as the doorman rushed to fetch servants, and soon a somberly attired butler emerged. He hurried to the carriage door with a large oilcloth umbrella to escort his master in from the dismal weather and was a bit perplexed to find yet another occupant in the carriage.

"Escort Miss McDowell in, Javits." Gareth gave a stern look to Jessica so she would not counter the name given her. "Then tell the housekeeper to send Lady Elizabeth to us in the library."

Once inside, Jessica welcomed the warm, glowing coals under the earl's noble Adams mantel. Though it was early summer, it was still cold with the rain. Outwardly calm, she waited with some trepidation to see what manner of person this Lady Elizabeth might be. She hoped the woman wouldn't take after her nephew!

Jessica's fears were soon laid to rest as a graceful, pretty woman rushed into the room, brushing abstractedly at what appeared to be bits of fluff clinging all over her gown. "Gareth! I've been so concerned; we'd expected you back days ago—" she began, not noticing Jessica.

The earl stared at her. "Aunt Bet, what on earth have you been into?"

She glanced down at her skirt and giggled. "It was the most amusing thing. You remember that old goose down mattress in the yellow suite? Well—oh!" She finally noticed Jessica standing off to the side. "Gareth, you have brought a guest!"

Gareth sighed. "Jessica, this is Lady Elizabeth, my aunt.

Aunt Bet, Miss Jessica Lynn McDowell, the niece of Laird Roland McDowell, of the Scottish estate I am settling." He gave Jessica a glance, warning her to keep quiet.

"Jessica. What a lovely name. I am so very sorry about your uncle, my dear. Have you brought her to stay in London with relatives?" she inquired of Gareth.

"Jessica has no other relatives. She shall be staying here as my—ward," he finally managed in a bit of a strangled voice, but Elizabeth paid no note.

"Oh, how sad, but we are delighted to have you with us!" the lady exclaimed. "It will be such fun to have a young person about." She smiled at Jessica.

"Heavens, you are scarcely old, Lady Elizabeth," Jessica said guilelessly, immediately delighted with Gareth's aunt.

"How sweet of you! And it's Aunt Bet, my dear. Come." She led Jessica over to the settee. "Gareth, ring for a tea tray, please love, while I get to know this child. Now, tell me about yourself. Gareth said nothing about any remaining relatives when he left for Scotland."

"She has been away at school." The earl looked again at Jessica as he answered, cutting off whatever she intended saying. "The solicitor who contacted me wasn't the laird's regular attorney and didn't know about her. Her parents are both deceased."

"How terrible!" Elizabeth patted Jessica's hand maternally. "But we shall be your family now, won't we, Gareth?" Fortunately, she continued speaking without waiting for a reply. "You shall have the blue suite. It overlooks the park and has a lovely view. The yellow is also very nice, but I'm afraid it's quite a mess right now. There was this feather mattress—"

"Aunt Bet," Gareth put in, "if I may interrupt, I'm sure you can tell Miss O'Don—uh, McDowell, of your escapades in due course. I would appreciate if if you would see to having her settled. Perhaps you might make appointments with your dressmaker and hairdresser—whatever is necessary for her to be presented this season." At his aunt's startled look, he rushed to explain. "I am certain it will be all right as it was only her uncle who died, and his demise is not generally known since he was in Scotland." He hoped that covered his aunt's very proper concern over the lack of a mourning period. He had no intention of housing the chit for that long! "Her uncle had plans for her to have a season—" Gareth's distaste of prevarication stopped him. Unable to meet Jessica's confused look, he changed his tactic. "You will agree with me, I am sure, that it will probably do the child much more good to be able to meet some young people and attend diverting events, rather than having to be closeted in mourning."

"How very thoughtful of you, Gareth. I'm sure you are quite right." Elizabeth had always considered the long mourning periods rather unnecessary. "If, of course, Jessica . . ." She looked over in concern at the girl.

"Of course, if you think so." Jessica agreed quietly, hiding her chagrin at this further evidence that the earl would do anything to have her off his hands. "I'm certain Uncle wouldn't have minded." *Especially under the circumstances,* she mentally added.

"I am so very glad you are with us, my dear! We shall soon have you quite into things. We can go to all the balls and soirees. This season shall be most delightful." Elizabeth chattered gaily, sweeping Jessica along into her own perpetual good humor. "You shall be so wonderful to dress! What marvelous hair. Isn't her hair absolutely wondrous, Gareth? A most unusual color! And freckles yet! But they are so becoming to you. They remind me of Kettle's puppy—the one you like, Gareth, with the speckles." She turned to the earl as he rolled his eyes in disbelief.

"Aunt Bet!" Gareth began testily, but Jessica only laughed, not at all upset by the comparison.

"You have puppies? I should love to see them!"

"Of course." Elizabeth smiled. "They are so dear. We'll go down after tea. They're in the kitchen because of the cool and dampness this week—"

"Ladies, I fear I must excuse myself as I have some matters to attend to." The earl decided he had had quite enough for one day.

"Certainly, Gareth, you run on along." Elizabeth waved him casually out the door as one might a restless boy, before turning back to the grinning Jessica. "Now my dear, where were we? Oh, I'm so very glad you are going to stay. I fear I must admit I have at times been bored to flinders with just Gareth and myself around. Oh, you mustn't misunderstand; he is a dear boy. But he can be so—stuffy—at times, if you know what I mean."

Jessica did. She couldn't help remarking on the difference between the two relatives.

"Well, I'm not a St. John. Naturally, they are all quite high of the instep. It is a very old title you understand," she added somewhat obliquely. "I'm the sister of Gareth's mother. We're Cavendish from Surry." She rattled on happily, giving Jessica, if not a definitive explanation, at least an all but complete and quite colorful feeling of the main characters involved.

Gareth, in the meantime, had retreated to his own quarters in relief. He ordered Javits to bring his port to his room, where he planned a peaceful hour before his own fire. After that time the women should have finished with their tea and left his library so he could see to neglected business. It had been poor planning on his part to have Aunt Bet meet Jessica there rather than in the parlor, but he could scarcely ask them to leave. On thinking of his aunt, Gareth shook his head in wonder. Though he loved her to death, it still amazed him at times what an absolute scatterbrain she could be! Well, the two of them should get along perfectly at any rate. He couldn't believe what Aunt Bet had actually said about the girl's freckles! Though it echoed his own thoughts, it wasn't the type of thing one ever expressed aloud. Although, amazingly enough, the girl hadn't seemed to mind at all, but rather had laughed! Gareth shuddered to imagine what Meredith would have done had someone compared her to a speckled pup.

Thoughts of Meredith made the earl frown. Tomorrow evening was her ball, and at the moment he could think of nothing he cared to do less than spend hours in an overcrowded ballroom. Meredith's mother was one of the worst for trying to have every name of society attend her parties, even though her home was not proportioned to hold crowds. The way Meredith adored parties, she was likely to be wanting them constantly, as her mother did. Gareth had to forcibly make himself think of his intended's beauty to raise his mood. Meredith by far outshone the other young ladies of her set in both beauty and social accomplishments. She epitomized the classic English beauty, with her porcelain complexion, golden hair and almost sapphire eyes. On meeting her, Gareth's first thought had been how lovely her portrait should be above his mantel. Now trying to visualize Meredith, for some reason a tan, freckled face with jade eyes came instead into his mind. The earl absently raised his glass to the fire. That was the color! The firelight reflected through the port in shades of red much like those of Jessica's hair. Surprised at his own thoughts, the earl carefully directed his mind to other matters.

After waiting the requisite hour, Gareth decided it should probably be safe to return to his library to look over mail from the past two weeks he'd been absent.

Apparently the women had gone on about other business, as the earl found the library empty. He settled contentedly in his favorite high backed chair before the fire and began opening the accumulated mail. His peace was soon disturbed, however, as the door was flung open and Jessica skipped in, quite unannounced.

"Look, Aunt Bet! The cook fetched me the speckled one! Isn't he just adorable!" She knelt happily beside Gareth's chair before glancing up. "Oh!" Jessica looked around in panic. "Uh, Aunt B—that is, Lady Elizabeth was here just a moment ago."

"She obviously isn't here now." Gareth found it difficult to be as curt as he should, faced with the appealing picture of a girl kneeling at his feet clutching a puppy. "And it is generally considered proper to knock before entering a room."

"I beg your pardon, Your Lordship." Jessica started to rise, but just then the puppy wiggled free and scurried beneath the earl's chair. Jessica made a desperate grab for it just as Elizabeth and the guests she had gone to escort from the vestibule entered the room.

"Jessica, Lady Summerwood and her daughter—" Elizabeth stopped in shock.

"What on earth?" Lady Summerwood exclaimed, staring at the confusion of skirts and petticoats as Jessica scuffled with the pup before pulling him out from under the earl's chair.

On hearing the exclamation, Jessica turned a startled countenance toward the guests, making a haphazard attempt to straighten her skirts and still hold onto the squirming puppy.

"Lord St. John!" Lady Summerwood's tone was horrified.

Gareth groaned and started to rise, only to discover that Jessica's skirts were entangled about his feet. "Jessica, would you mind returning that dog to the kitchen?" he finally managed, almost evenly.

"Yes, my lord." Jessica gave a frightened glance up at the earl, having come to recognize that dangerous tone in his voice, and quickly disentangled herself. With scarcely a look at the others, she scampered out with the puppy. Her exit was followed by a baleful glare from both the Summerwoods, and a somewhat bemused look from Elizabeth.

Gareth forced himself to turn calmly and address the women. "Well, Lady Summerwood, Meredith, an unexpected surprise."

"That is quite obvious!" Lady Summerwood harrumphed, but Elizabeth quickly interceded.

"Gareth, I must apologize! When I left the room but a moment ago, only Jessica was here," she said, trying to explain having allowed these two into the embarrassing situation.

"That is of no consequence, Aunt. Would you ladies care to have a seat?" Gareth carefully concealed his fury. That blamed girl had managed to do it to him again! Should he forever be plunged into these ridiculous situations by her?

"I think perhaps we would like an explanation first," Lady Summerwood declared haughtily.

Gareth found his fury increased at her presumption. The nerve of the woman! He raised a brow expressively. "An explanation, madam?" he asked quite coldly.

Lady Summerwood paled, realizing she had overstepped her bounds by calling down an earl, but Meredith, confident in her claims, leapt boldly in. "Yes, an explanation, Gareth. What on earth was that—serving wench—doing crawling about beneath your chair?"

His betrothed or not, Gareth refused to let any female challenge him in his own home. "Miss Summerwood, that was Miss Jessica McDowell, my young relative and ward, not a serving wench. If you will excuse me." He nodded curtly to them and stalked from the room. By God that had done it! He was going to find that girl and strangle her!

Lady Summerwood looked on in horror as the earl slammed the door shut behind him, fond visions of her daughter being Countess St. John fleeing at his wrath. "Meredith! How could you speak to the earl in such a manner?" she asked, conveniently forgetting that she had first confronted the man.

Meredith looked momentarily shaken but quickly collected herself, and with a defiant toss of her lovely head, snapped back, "Mother, I think perhaps we should take our leave."

"Yes, another time would be preferable to visit, I'm sure," Elizabeth agreed readily, having stood back aghast through the whole scene. *Well, it certainly isn't boring around here now*, she thought as she escorted the women out.

Mrs. Agnes, the cook, glanced briefly at Lord St. John's face as he stormed into the kitchen and wisely decided that she had business elsewhere. She callously abandoned Jessica to his wrath with only a hurried muttering about fetching more coal.

Jessica glanced up in terror at the earl as he towered over where she sat huddled with the puppies in her lap.

"I have never, *never* in my entire life found myself embroiled in such distasteful situations as those you have continually involved me in since our unfortunate introduction!" Gareth fairly bellowed at her. "Put those dogs down and stand up when I speak to you!"

Jessica quickly moved the pups back to their box and shakily stood up. "Sir, please, I'm sor—"

"I really don't care to hear your excuses!" Gareth interrupted her, unmoved by the tears streaming down her cheeks. "You are going to start behaving like something other than a haymarket hoyden, if I have to beat some sense into you!"

"Gareth!" Elizabeth gasped from the kitchen door.

Gareth contained his emotions with some effort. "Elizabeth, take Miss McDowell to her suite and see that she stays there," he growled, and strode from the kitchen without a backward glance at the convulsively sobbing girl.

It took Elizabeth almost an hour to calm the hiccuping child enough to elicit the happenings since Jessica had met the earl which had so incensed him. Elizabeth was sorely put not to laugh when she realized what her illustrious nephew had been subjected to, but she realized it wasn't amusing to the forlorn Jessica.

"I will not remain here, Lady Elizabeth! I cannot!" Jess hiccuped between sobs. "I should rather starve on the moors then remain in *his* house! The—the earl *hates* me, and I have done nothing!"

Elizabeth raised her brows, recalling all too clearly the startling sight of a female derriere beneath the froth of petticoats as the girl had crawled from beneath the earl's feet. Though she didn't particularly like the Summerwoods, as they had deemed to notice her only once Meredith had set her cap for Gareth. Nonetheless, she couldn't help but credit their shock on coming upon such a scene. Had she known Gareth was in the library, she would never have escorted them there, thinking merely to introduce them to Jessica. Heavens, what a hum! Never had she seen the earl in such a way!

"There, there, my dear. Of course the earl doesn't hate you." She tried to soothe the girl. "He was merely a bit distraught. He'll get over it." *In time,* she added mentally, though heaven only would know when.

Elizabeth finally got an exhausted Jessica out of her gown, into a soft cambric sleeping gown, and tucked into bed. Cook herself had brought Jessica a tray with a tempting dinner of powdered beef and syllabub lightly laced with brandy, "so the young miss would sleep." The servants had all, of course, heard the tale and swung to Jessica's side. It pleased them no end to hear of Miss Summerwood's set down by the earl, as none of them particularly liked her with all her "fine airs."

Once Jessica was safely asleep, Elizabeth went to find Gareth to see if she couldn't smooth things over. She discovered he had gone to White's, his favored St. James Street club, leaving word he would likely be very late returning.

Chapter Three

The Charley patrolling the Arlington neighborhood was just calling "Three o'clock and all's well," when Gareth finally rode back up his street. Gareth nodded to the familiar young lunker as he passed him and was greeted by a toothy, knowing grin and wave of the man's staff. Guessing at the other man's assumption, Gareth cynically realized word must not yet have gotten out that he'd released Bernadette, his latest and hopefully last, mistress.

Gareth dismissed his valet, who had waited up for him, and flung his own clothes off wearily. Still too agitated for sleep, he donned a long dressing robe and settled moodily before the remaining embers of the fire. He wasn't very concerned about Meredith and Lady Summerwood, knowing his title and fortune would bring them around. With more cynicism than conceit, he knew himself to be considered "the catch of the marriage mart." His real problem was that blamed child! Begrudgingly, he had to admit the predicaments she unerringly engendered were more innocent blunders than schemes contrived to embarrass. But how in the blazes could such a small bundle of femininity cause so many humiliating scenes?

With chagrin, the earl realized he had truly terrorized the child. The way he had yelled at her, he wouldn't be surprised if she tried to run away or do something equally foolish. Perhaps he should check to be certain she was all right.

With that thought in mind, Gareth headed down the hall to the blue suite where he'd heard his aunt was putting Jessica. With consternation, he found the door to the suite standing open, and a quick glance inside confirmed she was not in the bed. As he left the room he felt a draft and realized the glazed French doors to the upstairs balcony were likewise open.

"Good God!" he muttered. Surely she wouldn't do something that drastic. They were on the third floor! Gareth rushed to stare in expectant horror over the balcony's stone railing before sensing someone behind him. Turning, he found Jessica standing against the wall in only her sleeping gown, staring out into the night.

Gareth started to speak, then hesitated at the way she stood there clearly oblivious to everything. He walked closer and looked at her. The girl was sleepwalking! She didn't even realize he was there.

Recalling it was unwise to startle someone awake from that state, he refrained from touching her, merely saying her name softly. "Jessica?"

She turned and looked unseeingly in his direction. "Papa? Papa are you here?"

Gareth felt a pang of conscience. The poor lass had been through an awful lot these last days. "Come, child, you must return to bed." He guided her gently, but she swayed toward him trembling.

"I'm cold, Papa, and so tired."

Gareth felt her arm. The child was practically frozen! No telling how long she'd been standing outside in just her thin gown. Gareth easily lifted her, and holding her close against himself to warm her, carried her back inside. Jessica didn't awaken but merely slipped one arm about his neck, cuddling even closer.

As she nestled against his warmth Gareth stopped, finding himself suddenly filled with the startling urge to carry the young woman to his own room. He hesitated only a second, looking down at her, then shocked by his own thoughts, he headed determinedly to the blue suite.

Jessica's room was still warm from the evening fire, but he quickly tucked her under the coverlet, adding an extra comforter to her bed. Gareth shoveled more coal onto the embers and rekindled the fire. Turning, he stood for a long moment and looked at the sleeping girl as she lay there, her hair fanned in a subdued flame over the pillow.

Gareth had left the house early on some business, and it was almost noon before Elizabeth managed to corner him in his library and tow in the very reluctant Jessica. It had taken her all morning to convince the girl that the man wasn't really such an ogre, and a simple apology would put things to right again.

Both women were surprised at the earl's rather distracted acceptance of her halting apology. Gareth merely nodded and said, "The whole matter is perhaps best forgotten." He turned to his aunt. "Aunt Bet, as you recall, the Summerwoods' ball is tonight and despite the occurrences of yesterday, I'm afraid we are committed to attend. I have arranged for you to have the coach at your disposal, so you and Jessica might proceed to Bond Street to purchase a ball gown and whatever you need for this evening. You may as well begin replenishing Jessica's wardrobe for the season while you are there. Just put it on my accounts. I'll—apply it to the estate later," he added for Jessica's benefit, forestalling her protest, as he turned his attention dismissively back to his papers.

Elizabeth smiled at the girl as they turned to leave the library. "Monsieur Touraine, my hairdresser, is coming this evening. I described you to him this morning when he called for our usual appointment and he said your curls should be perfect for the new short style 'à la Greque'—"

"No!"

Both of the women turned, startled at Gareth's curt interruption. "Gareth?" Elizabeth questioned. "You did say you wished Jessica to see my hairdresser."

Gareth had spoken without thinking, the mere idea of Touraine cutting Jessica's masses of curls having elicited the response. "I, uh, really don't care for that new style of short hair. Have him leave the length alone," he said brusquely, again returning pointedly to his papers.

Elizabeth hesitated only a moment before ushering Jessica out.

"Why on earth should he care about my hair?" Jessica remarked once they were out of range.

"Oh, some men consider the new cut a bit forward," Elizabeth said, wondering herself why Gareth should have been the least bit interested. Perhaps there was hope yet he wouldn't wed that prim Meredith! She gave Jessica a speculative look. A pretty girl, but so—well, different. Not at all Gareth's usual style, not to mention her irrepressible habit of tumbling into trouble without the slightest provocation. She shook her head. No, it must have just been one of her nephew's odd quirks.

Jessica, always quick to rebound in spirits, set out to enjoy the day with Elizabeth. They first visited linendrapers, going to Elizabeth's favored Harding and Howell off Pall Mall, where jaconet, muslin, and cambric were chosen for morning gowns. Jessica delighted in a splendid length of emerald velvet for her very first riding habit. Elizabeth even insisted on some kersymere for a second habit, with gold bugle trimming to round it. To these treasures were added two lovely watered silks for future ball gowns, and the usual sarcenet and linen for pelisses.

From the linendrapers, they proceeded on to Bond Street to purchase a ball gown that could be altered for that evening. Elizabeth directed the carriage to the small shop of a French modiste she particularly liked.

"My dear, I'm afraid you must wear white this evening," Elizabeth said to forestall Jessica, who had headed instinctively to a display featuring a brilliant scarlet-and-white checked taffeta gown.

"White? Whatever for? I do so like colors."

"I know it's all silly, my child, but London society is very strict. Young girls simply must wear white to their first balls. I shall have to insist that you oblige me in these matters, as it is very easy to be cast from the pale of society by reason of the smallest indiscretions."

Jessica viewed the snow white frothy confections the modiste brought for approval in dismay. Then one of the young assistants brought an ivory satin gown from the rear.

"Oh . . . Aunt Bet! I love this one!"

Elizabeth had to agree that the rich cream color was indeed more complimentary to Jessica's coloration than the stark whites. And the delicately scalloped Brussels lace and seed pearls were lovely.

"It is *ravisante*!" the modiste exclaimed, standing back to survey the gown after buttoning Jessica into it. "And shall scarcely need any altering at all to fit mademoiselle."

"Absolutely delightful!" Elizabeth concurred happily, but Jessica was looking in the mirror a bit startled. "What is it, child? You don't like it?"

"It's lovely, but—I don't know." Jessica tugged unsuccessfully at the gown's bodice, which was scooped to show the soft swells of her breasts slightly. "I don't think it fits right, Aunt Bet. It shows . . ." she hesitated in embarrassment. "It shows *me*."

Elizabeth and the dressmaker exchanged smiles. "Mademoiselle is just from school, yes?" the proprietress rightly surmised.

"Yes." Elizabeth removed Jessica's hands from their unnecessary task. "Now dear, this dress is quite modest. Surely you don't think I would allow you to purchase it otherwise? You are just accustomed to your school dresses. I assure you you will see gowns with a much lower décolletage on the other girls tonight. It is the style."

"If you're certain." Jessica finally allowed herself to be convinced as she dearly loved the beautiful dress.

After picking out all the necessary accessories for her own ensemble, Jessica enthusiastically insisted on seeing that Aunt Bet selected an equally lovely gown. They finally agreed on one in a beautiful dusty rose, embroidered in silken catkins. The color brought a soft glow out in Elizabeth's complexion, making her look scarcely more than a girl herself.

"Oh my, this is dreadfully expensive!" Elizabeth worried, though obviously quite pleased with the selection. "Gareth shall doubtless choke when he gets this bill!" She hesitated a moment and then grinned at Jessica. "But then again, it shall serve him right for being such a tyrant to you last night. That was really not at all like Gareth," she commented thoughtfully.

After dressing later that evening, Jessica nervously surveyed herself in the full-length tortoiseshell mirror. This would be her first ball, and she was forced to go with the *earl*. Moreover, the ball was being given by that woman who had made all the fuss yesterday, making his lordship so angry with her. "Oh Aunt Bet, are you certain I look all right?" she inquired for the third time.

"You are quite lovely, child," Elizabeth assured her. Indeed she was, but in such a different way from the English girls that Elizabeth was concerned on how Jessica would "take," though she of course kept that thought to herself.

The hairdresser, after trying in vain to get Elizabeth to agree to the new Grecian cut for Jessica, had finally settled for the effect of the style by swooping her hair up to mass curls about her face, with the length in a brilliant cascade down the back. Small, cream-colored rose buds accented the red waves.

Elizabeth tried to cover Jessica's freckles with powder, but Jessica rebelled. "I feel as if I have on a mask!" She frowned, and washed off the offending makeup. "I don't care what anyonc thinks of my freckles anyway!" Jessica had firmly decided after her last episode with the earl that men were simply not worth the catching, and almost hoped her freckles would affront them.

Gareth had stressed that Elizabeth was to carefully tutor Jessica in behavior for the evening, hoping to avoid yet another catastrophe. So as they dressed, Aunt Bet carefully ran through the prescribed social amenities.

"Oh dear, I'll never remember all of that," Jessica complained as she was instructed once again on protocol. "Why must there be so many rules for everything?"

"Now you need not worry that Gareth is escorting us." Elizabeth guessed Jessica's main fear. "As he is engaged to Meredith, he shall spend most of his time with her, so you shall be with me. I will be there for directions if you get confused about anything."

Jessica said nothing but was still concerned about the earl's proximity, convinced he would manage to find some complaint.

His lordship certainly had no cause to complain as he watched the two ladies descend the stairs to where he waited for them in the foyer.

The gown and new hairstyle had turned Jessica's girlish image into that of a strikingly beautiful young woman, Gareth acknowledged in surprise. Different in appearance from most debutantes, but quite lovely. Well, if the lads at the ball weren't put off by her unique coloring, she would certainly not lack for suitors, Gareth decided as he considered her. He'd likely have her off his hands quicker than he'd imagined. As he escorted them to the carriage, he refused to question why that possibility didn't exactly bring to him the expected satisfaction.

Jessica settled herself opposite Gareth in his plush emerald and silver brougham. The earl politely complimented both ladies on their appearance, but Jessica had felt him glance at her several times and nervously feared he disapproved of something yet again.

Gareth actually was a bit bewildered by her metamorphosis and her odd, new allurement. It was hard to tell exactly what it was about Jessica that was so—intriguing, was perhaps the word. The hair, of course, for one thing. Then there were her almost emerald eyes. Her mouth, really too generous to fit the accepted standard of the "Cupid's bow," but somehow very, very—

Gareth glanced away from his study as she looked up anxiously at him. He resumed it again, however, as his aunt directed Jessica's attention to some scenery they passed, and found his eyes coming to rest on the soft lace lying against the curves of the girl's breast. A vision of the young bucks dancing with her tonight and doubtless enjoying the same view rose in his mind, and the earl frowned.

"Is something wrong, Gareth?" Elizabeth had caught his last glance at Jessica and the frown, and anxiously studied the girl, but she appeared quite acceptable.

Gareth looked critically back at Jessica. "Don't you feel the décolletage of that gown is a bit extreme for a girl her age, Aunt?"

Jessica blushed painfully as her hand fluttered to her breast. "Oh, Aunt Bet! I told you I thought it was too low!" she cried in mortification.

"Gareth!" Elizabeth said sharply. "Hush, child. There is nothing at all immodest about your gown. Whatever has come over you, Gareth? For heaven's sake, at the duke's ball last month, your own Meredith's dress was cut twice as low and you didn't even seem to notice!"

Gareth had actually, and with some annoyance, as Meredith had a way of using her status as "society's pet" for carte blanche and got away with more than the other young ladies. Somehow Meredith's overexposure of pearly skin had no effect on him other than the mild annoyance. "Meredith is older than Jessica," Gareth merely stated.

"Oh, humbug. I believe you're taking your status as Jessica's guardian overly serious. The girl is old enough to wear adult clothes. And Jessica"—she turned back to the girl—"there is nothing wrong with the cut of your gown. You'll see when we get to the ball. You look at what the other girls are wearing." Elizabeth frowned quellingly at Gareth for making the child even more nervous than she had been.

All too soon for Jessica, they arrived. "Lord St. John, Earl of Cantonley. Lady Elizabeth Trenton. Miss Jessica McDowell," the staid butler intoned as the trio entered the press of the already crowded room.

A hush fell over the gathering as most eyes turned toward the entry. Jessica edged nearer Elizabeth.

"Smile, dear," Elizabeth whispered under her breath as their hostess swept down upon them.

"We are so honored, Lord St. John!" Lady Summerwood gushed, terribly relieved that he had still come despite the events of the previous day. "And, oh Elizabeth, what a marvelous gown! And this, of course, is your delightful ward!" She smiled sweetly at Jessica. "I'm so sorry we had to leave before getting to properly meet you yesterday, my dear, but I'm afraid my Meredith confessed to a terrible megrim," she improvised by way of excuse. "The child has really overtaxed herself this season. She is just in such demand! It shall be such a burden from my mind when she is properly settled with a husband to look after her." Lady Summerwood fluttered her fan with a coquettish glance at the earl.

The object of the conversation herself came up behind her mother. "Mother! Such talk." Meredith curtsied charmingly to Gareth. "My lord. Lady Elizabeth." She turned back to Gareth. "I do apologize for leaving abruptly yesterday," she said prettily, "but I'm afraid Mama is right—I had truly overdone." The St. John emerald caught the light and accented the delicate hand she so beseechingly placed on Gareth's arm.

"Think nothing of it," he said with cynical amusement, and turned to Jessica, whom Meredith had ignored. "I would like to present my ward. I don't believe you met her yesterday. Miss Jessica McDowell, the Honorable Meredith Summerwood."

Jessica smiled rather uncertainly as the other girl looked her over. "Why, what a charming child!" Meredith enthused, with a flirtatious glance at Gareth. "I am so pleased you could come to my ball, Miss McDowell. Lady Elizabeth, you must take her and introduce her to the younger set of boys and girls," she continued sweetly.

Lady Summerwood, seeing the annoyance spring into Aunt Bet's eyes, moved forward to prevent disaster. "Meredith, dear, why don't you entertain the earl? Elizabeth and I shall take Jessica about and introduce her."

Gareth firmly told himself that he should be relieved to have the chit off his hands for a while and he turned his attention to Meredith. She was, after all, his choice to be Cantonley's next countess.

"My lord," Meredith said and pouted prettily up at him,

with assumed shyness, from beneath long lashes, "you have not said a word about my new gown, after I expressly chose it for your pleasure."

Gareth looked down at her. "As always, my dear, you look quite lovely." As indeed she did—a picture of peaches and cream perfection. Gareth could think of no reason to fault his choice for a bride, though he didn't believe he'd finally set a firm date with Lord Summerwood tonight as he'd originally planned. Meredith was a bit overconfident, as evidenced by her daring yesterday. It would do her good to be put off for a while.

The earl escorted Meredith into the crowded room, scarcely hearing her continuing chatter about her latest acquisitions from some new modiste.

Gareth led Meredith in the second coterie of dances, already tired of the crush and the twittering of inconsequential conversations. He had lost sight of Aunt Bet and Jessica some time before and now glanced about to see if he could spot them.

"Why, there's your young relative," Meredith remarked just then. "I do believe she's dancing with one of the officers from the garrison."

The earl watched as the other couple executed the formal steps of the quadrille, the young officer seeming quite entranced with Jessica. He then scanned the room and spotted his aunt in lively conversation with some of her friends.

When the dance ended, he led Meredith back to her mother to await her next partner, and excusing himself returned to where the gentleman was talking to Jessica.

As the earl approached, he realized with amazement that the two were discussing the merits and pitfalls of the feudal system.

"I have a friend, a sea captain, who told me that in

America anyone can go and claim land," the lieutenant was just telling Jessica as Gareth came up.

"Assuming you don't mind fighting off the savages," Gareth said acerbically, unreasonably annoyed that they should be having such a conversation, while he had been regaled the last hour by nothing but meaningless *on dits*. The couple halted awkwardly in their conversation at his remark.

Jessica collected herself enough to introduce her escort. "Lord St. John, this is Lieutenant Gantry—Lieutenant, my guardian, the Earl of Cantonley."

The two gentlemen acknowledged the introduction and the lieutenant, overawed by the earl, decided on a temporary retreat. "It has been delightful, Miss McDowell," he said, and bowed lingeringly over her hand. "Might I have the pleasure of escorting you to supper?"

"Thank you, sir, but I'm afraid your friend, Lieutenant Landers, previously asked."

"My misfortune. Perhaps you might save me another dance later?"

"I should be pleased." Jessica smiled as he signed her card for one of the later country sets.

Gareth noticed her card was almost full, but at a glance, most of the names appeared to have rank before them, designating the officer's group. He wondered vaguely why none of his peers seemed to have noticed her. Seeing the next dance on her card was vacant, he offered Jessica his arm. "Perhaps, Miss McDowell, you might honor me with this dance?"

Jessica looked at him in rather startled surprise. "Sir, the next dance is a waltz, and Aunt Elizabeth said—"

The earl had not realized it was a waltz. He hesitated but a moment and then led her onto the floor. "As your guardian it is acceptable for you to waltz with me," he said firmly.

"But, Your Lordship, I am not really versed in the steps of the dance having never—"

"It's a simple step actually—I'll show you." He surprised her by smiling down as he led her across the floor. "Here, we shall move over by the patio where there isn't such a press, and you needn't look so startled," the earl said soothingly as he showed Jessica the dance position. "I can't really be all that fearsome."

"You can indeed!" Jessica retorted, but managed to relax under his joking tone. "You quite horrified me again, only last night!"

"Only after you first horrified me!" he quipped, and she couldn't help but giggle.

"Who would ever expect Lady and Miss Summerwood to come in at exactly that moment?"

The earl found himself chuckling, although he commented dryly that it was not a matter he cared to discuss. Adroitly changing the subject, Gareth explained the dance as he guided her through the steps. "It's quite easy, see? One, two, three—one, two, three—"

Jessica quickly caught onto the rhythm and smiled up at him. "This is a delightful dance. It seems so graceful. Why have I never heard of it?"

"It has only recently been introduced even in London. Countess Lieven brought it to the *ton* first, dancing at Almack's with Palmerston." He realized Jessica had no idea who he was speaking of and so elaborated. "The countess is the wife of our Russian ambassador, and manages to do things others could not do without social disgrace. The *ton* lionizes her because of her family lineage and rather extraordinary beauty."

Inexplicably Jessica found herself disliking this Lieven woman. "And you, sir, you find her—beautiful, this countess?"

He glanced down at her curiously. "She is quite lovely—

at least to look upon." He continued without elaboration, "Lord Palmerston is one of her beaux. I expect they considered it a lark to dare such a dance, but it has become popular."

"Beaux?" Jessica frowned, caught by the term. "I thought you said the countess was married to—"

"Friends." Gareth corrected his gaff and carefully redirected the subject. "Although the dance is now accepted, it is still considered improper for young girls until they receive permission from the matriarchs of Almack's."

As Elizabeth had explained some of the mysteries of the famed Almack's, Jessica passed over that. She studied their feet carefully and said, "I really cannot see what might be considered wrong with such a dance."

Gareth grinned. "It is not the actual steps that are deemed objectionable, but the closeness with which one dances to one's partner."

"Oh!" Jessica missed a step as she looked at the earl's chest, and was momentarily startled to notice for the first time how close they were.

Gareth, restraining a smile, smoothly continued as though he had not noticed her embarrassment. "Lady Jersey, one of the prime matriarchs of Almack's, has actually been known to carry a ruler about the dance floor to insure that the young ladies and gentlemen remain the prescribed fourteen inches apart at all times."

"Fourteen inches?" Jessica looked down seriously. "Oh, dear. Sir, I really don't believe we are quite fourteen inches apart—do you?"

Gareth, having his gaze thus innocently directed to her soft breasts, indeed quite closer than the prescribed distance, found himself momentarily distracted from the dance, and unthinkingly executed a turn unfamiliar to his partner.

"Sir!" Jessica protested as she quite lost her balance in

the dance step. Laughing, she momentarily leaned against the earl's broad chest for support.

"My apologies." Gareth laughed also, guiding her back away from him with some regret. "I forgot. Here, I'll show you slowly." He waltzed her through the turn again, totally oblivious to the many stares of the other couples. In fact, as he instructed her, neither of them were the slightest bit aware of anyone else until the music ended.

"My dear, perhaps you would like some punch?" Aunt Bet said as she retrieved Jessica from Gareth's side the moment the music stopped. Whatever was the man thinking? Waltzing with the child like that! The whole room had been staring, and Meredith was positively seething.

"Oh, I suppose," Jessica said reluctantly, and turned back to Gareth. "That was quite fun, my lord. Will you dance with me again?" she asked guilelessly, as Aunt Bet rolled her eyes.

The earl, however, only chuckled. "I think not, brat, it appears we have all but scandalized Aunt Bet. And you really should allow the gentleman to ask," he added as an afterthought, before leaving her in his aunt's hands.

Elizabeth shook her head in wonder as she reproached Jessica.

"But Aunt, Lord St. John said it was all right," Jessica told her, an argument the woman assuredly found difficult to counter.

The earl dutifully returned to Meredith. He read, with annoyance, her displeasure at the preceding dance, but overlooked it as, at least this time, she kept enough presence of mind not to risk calling him down.

Lady Summerwood was dismayed at what might follow from the dance she had witnessed. She quickly cornered her husband and insisted that he speak to the earl. "Edward, you really must have Lord St. John declare his intentions toward Meredith. This dragging the matter out is very upsetting to the child." She didn't mention her real fears that the earl might change his mind.

Lord Summerwood had been in the card room with his friends and witnessed none of the foregoing spectacle. Gareth was his friend, and he would certainly not have pressed the earl had he suspicioned it untimely. But to accommodate his wife, Lord Summerwood agreed to see if he couldn't take the earl aside for a talk.

Gareth was glad for an excuse to leave the company of the pouting Meredith, and on seeing the viscount approach, addressed the gentleman first. "Summerwood, I've wondered that I haven't seen you this evening. Perhaps you'll excuse me, my dear," he said casually to Meredith before joining her father. Gareth carefully headed back for the card room as he conversed with Lord Summerwood, although fully aware that the man was hinting he'd like a more private conference.

Chapter Four

Meredith's annoyance was somewhat eased when Gareth once again appeared at her side to escort her to supper. Her mother was right, for once. It was really time his lordship set a wedding date. She was definitely not going to allow her friends to laugh at her behind her back because of some country miss. Perhaps she had ignored Gareth too much, but it was such fun to flirt with all her suitors. Gareth, however, had tarried long enough. Tonight she would turn on all her charm, she decided serenely. That couldn't help but bring him up to snuff!

The earl's previous impatience with Meredith dissolved as she set out to please him so prettily. No man could avoid being distracted by the flirtatious glances and soft pouting lips of such a beauty.

Meredith chatted gaily during dinner, filling his lordship in on all the latest *on dits* she was sure he would be interested in. "Young Douglas, I've heard, was quite into his cups. I do believe that is the fourth phaeton he's all but destroyed. His Grace must be thoroughly put out with him." She laughingly leaned toward him, smugly noticing as his eyes wandered to her revealed cleavage.

Gareth brought his mind to the content of the conversation, the duke's rakehell of a younger son, Douglas, having recently outbid him on a delightful pair of Tattersal's bays. "What cattle was he driving?"

"What?" Meredith paused in surprise. Who cared about horses? "Oh, those new ones he recently purchased, I believe. No matter, they've decided to run the race again. Of course, no one is supposed to know." She chatted on until Gareth again interrupted.

"Were either of the animals injured?"

"What animals?" She looked at him in confusion, having already forgotten his previous question.

"The bays, Meredith," Gareth said impatiently. "That was the pair the scamp outbid me on last month."

"A pity." She feigned concern. "I seem to recall one had to be destroyed. Oh, but let's not talk about such morbid things." She gave a delightful little shudder as she looked beseechingly up at him.

Gareth forced himself to draw his thoughts back to the woman at his side as they finished dinner.

When they returned to the ballroom, Meredith decided it was time for her to make an offer, a *fait accompli*. She would allow the earl to kiss her. He had scarce been able to keep his eyes from her lips all evening, except when they wandered lower. She smiled to herself. "Isn't it exceedingly warm tonight, my lord?" She fluttered her fan demurely. "I cannot imagine why Mother insists on having quite so many people, except that she says she just can't bear to disappoint anyone." She glanced up provocatively.

The earl, having no qualms about being lured into the gardens, willingly said, "Perhaps you would enjoy a stroll outside?"

Meredith, with proper maidenly blushes, agreed, adding, "Mother's prize roses are in bloom just now. I should love for you to see them."

"I would be delighted." Gareth led her into the garden, not surprised at all to find the prize roses in a very secluded section.

He was, however, surprised at his "chaste" Meredith's reaction to what should have been, but his experience told him was not, her first kiss. Though she sighed in his arms, and whispered that she had never imagined this first experience could be so wonderful, Gareth knew she lied. He found himself taking a less tolerant view of her constant flirtations with whichever man was near. Even though it was accepted in their society, when husbands and wives discreetly took lovers once the heirs were established, Gareth found the idea distasteful. He certainly had no intention of having such a wife.

Meredith was openly disappointed when Gareth did not seek to keep her in the gardens longer. Remarking that they mustn't tarnish her reputation, he led her back to the ballroom. She wasn't overly concerned, though. Content that he was physically attracted to her, she was certain that he would wish a wedding date established soon.

Gareth found himself strangely at odds with himself. He didn't understand his reluctance to make a final commitment to Meredith. She was undeniably beautiful, of impeccable lineage, conversant in all the social graces, and even physically stimulating. What more could he possibly desire?

The earl remained attentively at Meredith's side until Elizabeth sought him out later.

"Gareth," she said, drawing him aside, "I believe we should take Jessica home. She seems to be getting a fever."

"A fever?" He looked over at the girl. "She does appear

flushed." He walked over and touched Jessica's cheek, finding it exceedingly warm.

"I'm sorry, Your Lordship. I hate to interrupt your evening. I'm sure Aunt Bet can see me home—" Jessica began apologetically just as Meredith came up and hooked her arm possessively through Gareth's.

"Poor Jessica. You do look ill. Lady Elizabeth should take you home immediately." Meredith had no intention of letting him leave her party this early. "My lord, would you like me to have Father arrange one of our coaches so your carriage may stay on?"

The earl patted Meredith's hand absently before removing it from his arm. "I think not. I shall see them home myself. You will please extend my apologies to your parents?" he added, ushering the ladies out before an indignant Meredith could protest further.

Gareth frowned in concern when Jessica began shivering as they waited for his coach to come around. She had doubtless caught a chill out on the balcony the night before as he'd feared she might. "Here, child." He removed his multitiered cape and wrapped it about her as they entered the carriage. Once inside, much to his aunt's surprise, he drew Jessica next to him to warm her as they drove.

"I wonder where she caught such a chill?" Elizabeth said with concern as Jessica dozed against Gareth's shoulder.

"She has been under a strain with all the happenings of late. I should probably not have allowed her to attend the ball tonight."

"She was having a delightful time," Elizabeth commented, "though it seemed odd that only the young officers approached her."

Gareth frowned thoughtfully, falling silent until they reached his townhouse.

"Jessica?" Elizabeth leaned over to waken the girl, but

Gareth shook his head, and lifting her easily, carried her out.

"Go to Doctor Thomason, and bring him back here directly," the earl ordered his coachman, as Jessica shivered yet again.

Later both Gareth and Elizabeth stood by impatiently as the doctor examined Jessica. "I believe it to be just a chill she has taken," he said finally. "She doubtless has become overworn." Gareth had confided the events of the last days to him, minus the episode on the balcony. "You must keep her in bed for several days and give her plenty of nourishing liquids. She's young and healthy. I imagine she'll repair quickly, but it's best not to take any chances."

Elizabeth wanted to sit up with Jessica, but Gareth forbade it. "You've had a long day yourself, Aunt Bet. I'll have Javits assign a couple of the housemaids to take turns watching over her."

The housemaids assigned were surprised when the earl himself came and checked on the young mistress several times even though with the laudanum the doctor had given her, she slept through the night without awakening.

Gareth's patience thinned quickly the following day, when not one but four hopeful young officers presented themselves on his doorstep requesting permission to call upon Jessica. He managed to remain more polite than he felt as he sent them all on their way, with the information that she would be confined for at least a week.

Jessica herself was rather amazed when numerous bouquets arrived during the day from young men she had met. "Good heavens," she remarked to Elizabeth, "is it one of London's odd social requirements that you must send flowers to all the girls you dance with?"

Elizabeth laughed. "No, my dear. It is merely a sign that they like you. Why, Gareth's been turning young men from the door all day."

"Oh," she said a bit pensively, "I suppose he is pleased that one of them may perhaps wish to marry me and take me off his hands."

"Jessica, I'm sure that is not so at all. Why Gareth was very concerned about you last night—and didn't you have a pleasant dance together?"

"That is true," she agreed, not mentioning her disappointment that he hadn't approached her again the whole ball.

"By chance, are you interested in any of the young men?" Elizabeth smiled, attempting to lighten her mood.

"Oh, they were all quite nice," Jessica replied distractedly, "but I don't think I could . . ."

"Yes, what is it, child?" Aunt Bet queried in concern, noting Jessica's sudden agitation.

"Well, you should love someone to marry them," she said finally looking up at Elizabeth. "I could not just—oh, Aunt Bet, the earl would not insist that I—"

"There now, child." Elizabeth restrained a smile on realizing the source of the girl's horror. "Gareth is not going to drag you to the altar with the first man who asks. Surely you must give him more credit than that."

"Yes," Jessica agreed hesitantly. After all, he had seemed much nicer last night.

"And now what other Cheltingham drama is that nimble imagination of yours contriving?" Elizabeth teased to lighten the girl's mood.

Jessica smiled despite herself. "Aunt Bet, how do you know when you love someone?" she asked thoughtfully.

Elizabeth relaxed at this typical question. "You simply know. I don't think anyone else can adequately explain the feeling to you. But you can believe me that you will know. It may be that you will come to love your husband only after you are married. It is not necessarily expected that you fall in love first."

"I could never marry someone I didn't love," Jessica protested. "What if you did, and then did not fall in love with him? What if—if you fell in love with someone else?"

Elizabeth blithely soothed the girl's concern, then insisted she get some rest. After leaving, however, she considered Jessica's question, thinking how often the arranged marriages and marriages based upon titles and lineages were loveless. Her own marriage had been to a man that she loved only because her family, more understanding than most, had allowed her the choice. Donald had been a young officer, really quite beneath her station, but they had fallen in love—and had five wonderful years before he was killed in battle.

Jessica slept through most of the first day from the fever, but by the second day of forced rest, began to get quite edgy.

"Aunt Bet, I really feel quite fine," she said, and tried unsuccessfully to stifle a sneeze. "Surely I can get up. Could we just go for a walk in the park?"

"No, my dear," Elizabeth chided, "not with you sneezing and sniffling like that. I'll tell you what, I have some shopping to do and plan to stop by the circulating library. I'll bring you something to read when I return."

Jessica had to settle for that and named a couple of the recently published novels she had not yet read. "Does the earl subscribe to any monthlies?" she asked hopefully, realizing it likely would be some time before Aunt Bet got back.

"Well, his newspapers come here, but he has most of his monthly journals sent to Cantonley." Elizabeth wondered at the girl's interest.

"Do you suppose I could borrow some of his papers to read until you come back? Only, of course, if you think he wouldn't mind." Jessica was determined she wasn't going to do anything else to annoy the earl. In fact, just that morning while thinking on the matter, she had mentally vowed to become the very epitome of decorum from now on.

After Elizabeth left to fetch the papers, Jessica leapt out of bed and went over to the mirror. She could be every bit as prim as the earl's simpering Meredith, and then perhaps he wouldn't be so anxious to marry her off. She conscientiously buttoned her robe, brushed her hair, and tied it back with a large bow. Then after practicing what she considered a sweetly serious expression for a moment, was sedately returning to the bed when Elizabeth came back.

"Here, child, I brought you these." Elizabeth stopped, looking at Jessica in consternation. "Is something wrong?"

Jessica assumed an attitude of lofty astonishment. "Of course not, Aunt Elizabeth, I am quite fine actually."

"Aunt Elizabeth? Oh dear, are you feeling unwelcome again? Don't tell me Gareth's—"

Jessica couldn't help but giggle, and giving up, ran over and hugged the other woman. "Obviously I should not try to cozen you. You know me too well already, Aunt Bet. That was for His Lordship's benefit."

At Elizabeth's puzzled look she elaborated. "I was practicing being like those 'exemplary' young women of the *ton*. I am determined that I shall not cause His Lordship any further embarrassments. I shall become the very essence of propriety," she announced theatrically as she flopped enthusiastically onto the bed.

"The essence of propriety?" Elizabeth was understandably confused at the conflicting evidence of the girl's words and actions.

"Yes. I shall be as sweet and demure as that silly Meredith, since that's what men seem to like. And then the earl won't be so eager for me to leave and get married."

"Jessica, Gareth really isn't just trying to get rid of you. You must not think that—although I am sure that he will appreciate your concern," Elizabeth hastened to add, not wishing to discourage the girl. "However, you have a charming personality, and neither Gareth nor I should wish you to change."

"Oh, I won't really ever change," Jessica assured her seriously, "except in His Lordship's presence. I'm quite adept at acting, you see. I was in all the school plays. Of course, everyone was," she admitted honestly, "as there weren't that many of us, but I think I have a real talent for drama. In fact, I believe I could do well on stage. Don't you think so?"

"Oh dear." Elizabeth couldn't help but laugh. "No doubt at all. However, I do hope you shall prove wise enough never to suggest such a thing within Gareth's earshot. It is not at all appropriate for young ladies to go on stage!"

"No?" Jessica sighed regretfully. "Well, you'll be proud of me anyway, you'll see." She sat up decorously and arranged the papers with prim neatness about her. "Now, run along, dear Elizabeth," she said with a matronly air. "I shall be fine here perusing my papers."

Elizabeth broke out laughing. "Jessica, you are such fun to have about. Now don't get up while I'm gone, just ring for one of the servants should you be in need of anything."

It was some time later when the earl returned to his library. "Javits," he called to his butler, "have you seen the last issues of the *Examiner*? I thought certain I left them right here."

"Lady Trenton took the papers up to the young miss, sir. She thought you would be through with them. Shall I retrieve them for you?"

"That won't be necessary. I was going up to check on Miss McDowell anyway." There was an article on the new tariffs he had not had time to digest thoroughly, and he wished to discuss it with some of the members of the House of Lords who were coming to dinner that night.

Jessica had long since forgotten her intentions to behave with decorum as she sat cross-legged on the bed, her robe tucked up out of the way, and her curls again falling riotously about her shoulders. The once neat newspaper was scattered everywhere about her as she excitedly followed a particular set of articles through several issues with scissors poised. Thus engrossed, she only half heard the knock on her door.

"Come in," Jessica invited automatically, not even looking up as the door opened.

Gareth stood in stunned silence for some seconds before Jessica glanced up and saw him. "Your Lordship." She smiled welcomingly before his dark expression sank in, and looking down, she hastily assumed a more ladylike position. "I was just clipping some articles out of these papers," she frantically began to explain.

"Clipping!" He forgot the previous scene in his dismay, and quickly moved over. He yanked up one of the papers, revealing, as he feared, a large hole. "Who said you might destroy my newspapers?" Gareth said through clenched teeth, making a concerted effort to remain calm.

"Oh dear, you aren't going to yell again, are you?" Jessica asked nervously.

Gareth glowered at her. "I save my papers because they often contain articles to which I wish to refer. In fact, I came up here intending to review a recent article on tariffs"—he gathered several of the scattered sheets in exasperation—"assuming I can find the article still in one piece."

"Tariffs?" Jessica looked around quickly. "Oh, I remember, on landowners for that new road surface McAdam designed. I read that. It was well written and it seemed like such a good idea." She missed his surprised look as she leaned over the side of the bed. "It is over here I think."

Retrieving several sheets from the floor, she sat back up. "Ah, see, I haven't cut these at all."

"Marvelous," Gareth said sarcastically, taking the papers from her hands. "Is it too much to hope that the rest of this edition might also be available?"

Jessica glanced at him a little uncertainly as she quickly sorted out one set of sheets and handed them to him expectantly. "Here."

"In chronological order, if you don't mind." He tossed the one he held back onto the stack.

Jessica sighed as she re-sorted and neatly folded the papers together while he watched.

"I assume you are feeling more like yourself?" Gareth inquired pointedly, as he sat down on the side of the bed and glanced at the articles she'd cut out.

Jessica grimaced at his obvious meaning, remembering belatedly her intentions of impressing him. "Yes, I am really quite recovered," she assured him, immediately belying the claim with a sneeze. She groped among the tangled bedclothes for her handkerchief until Gareth resignedly handed her his own.

She didn't bother attempting to return it to him.

"Is there a particular reason you wish to save articles on highwaymen?" he inquired, observing the titles on the clipped articles.

"Not just any highwaymen." Jessica eagerly gathered together her other clippings, and forgetting her nervousness, moved over to show him. "See how strange this series of robberies is on the coastal highway?"

Gareth took the offered clippings and glanced through them. "The 'gentlemen bandits'? Yes, they are a pair who have escaped capture for the while, but highwaymen along that stretch aren't particularly rare. Actually, that is in Sussex near where Cantonley lies. Some of the robberies have even taken place on my land. As I am the magistrate of the area, I have been following them. In fact, my high sheriff is having people watch that road just now."

"Your lands?" Jessica couldn't believe her luck. "Then doesn't it strike you as strange, this regular pattern in the robberies? See, they only rob about the same time—never exactly, mind you, only close—mid-morning or evening, and then simply vanish. Also, they have never harmed anyone, nor have they taken so much as a shilling from the poor."

"Hmm." Gareth smiled at her excitement as he flipped through the articles again. "Yes, that's why they've been dubbed 'gentlemen,' though robbing anyone of anything should abolish their right to such a title."

"Well, I suppose," she agreed dubiously, but Gareth didn't notice, as he was reading one of the articles.

"The times do seem to be rather predictable," he mused, "though dusk is a likely time for any robbery. However I must admit these mid-morning times are a bit odd. But then again, thieves are a different lot and can scarcely be expected to act logically," he concluded, setting the articles back down.

"What about their vanishing? Isn't that mysterious?" Jessica persisted, disappointment at his lack of interest.

Gareth chuckled. "I'm sure there is some reasonable explanation. However, since you're obviously determined to make more of all this, discuss it with Aunt Bet—there's nothing she loves better than a mystery. Perhaps the two of you can solve the problem for me." He rose. "However, for the nonce I would appreciate you arranging what's left of my papers back in good order. I do not mind your borrowing them, but I must insist in the future that they be returned intact." He softened the order with a playful tousle of her curls as he left.

Jessica sat very still for a few seconds after the door closed behind the earl. She reached up and touched her own hair tentatively. What a very strange feeling it was to have his lordship's hand in her hair like that. It was difficult to describe, but it evoked a warm sensation much like when she had held Kettle's puppy—but not quite. She wished he hadn't left so quickly, then grinned at her own thoughts. Usually she was glad when he left, so that she could relax.

Jessica turned her thoughts away and quickly straightened up the scattered papers, then resumed the decorous pose for Elizabeth's sake. She hoped the earl wouldn't say anything about how he had found her earlier. Next time she would remember.

When Elizabeth returned, Jessica immediately told her about the mysterious highwaymen. Just as Gareth had predicted, she was instantly excited. "It's like you say, there is something significant about those times, mid-morning and dusk, but I can't imagine what. The only things I can think of that are always about a dozen hours apart like that are the tides at Cantonley."

"Tides! Why that's it! I'd be willing to wager that it is high tide mid-morning and dusk there this time of month."

Elizabeth looked at the girl in surprise. "Why yes, I believe you're right. But whatever does that have to do with highwaymen?"

"That is how they are vanishing so mysteriously—by ship. There must be a river they can use to sail out to the ocean. Since they ride horses, no one has thought to imagine them leaving by sea."

"That's ingenious, Jesse," Elizabeth agreed enthusiastically. "Why, it says right here, they have searched all the roads and inns of the area after each robbery with no apparent success. It doesn't mention a thing about checking the coast! There is a river from Baker's Inlet that is fairly wide and deep. Something the size of a private sloop could easily sail up it far enough to hide. I do believe it's right in the area of the robberies, too."

"Does the earl have a map of this area?"

"I think he should. Baker's Inlet is on Gareth's land; in fact, not far from the estate itself. I know he has maps of all the land and most likely charts of the waterways also, since he has his own sloop." Elizabeth suddenly paused long enough to realize the articles they had been studying were cut from the newspapers. "Oh my, Jessica, I don't know what Gareth's going to say about your cutting up his paper."

"He already has."

"Has what?"

"Said. About my cutting it up. He came in a while ago to get some of the papers back, but he didn't get too upset," Jessica added quickly.

"Are you sure he wasn't angry?" Elizabeth inquired anxiously, hoping Jessica hadn't done something else to incur her nephew's disdain. "Gareth's very particular about his papers and books. I really should have thought to warn you, but I hadn't expected you would cut them up."

"Well, he was a little annoyed. But I promised not to do it again."

Elizabeth relaxed. "Perhaps your improved image really did impress him then." Elizabeth smiled at Jessica's prim pose. "Did he say anything about the new 'Miss Essence of Propriety'?"

"Well, not actually," Jessica said evasively. "Why don't we go down to his library and try to find the maps?" she asked, quickly changing the subject.

"Not *we*, Miss McDowell." Elizabeth gently pushed the girl back. "I'll go see what I can find, and you stay right here and get back under the covers."

"Maps?" Gareth asked distractedly when interrupted from his work by Elizabeth. "Whatever do you want a map of Cantonley lands for?"

"Well, Jessica is reading these—" she began, and then Gareth chuckled.

"Oh, yes. Her highwayman mystery. You doubtless wish to chart where the robberies are taking place."

"Yes. Oh, and I'm really sorry about her clipping from your journals. I should have told her that you saved them."

"I'm afraid no one can quite anticipate Jessica," Gareth commented. "Perhaps this mystery will keep her out of mischief for a while anyway." He rose and opened a cabinet, revealing neatly labeled cubicles. "I keep the majority of Cantonley's papers on the estate; however, there is an abbreviated set of maps here. Those for the area you are interested in will be in the file entitled 'Southeast Quadrant.' " He gestured to one labeled section. "You may take the ones you wish to study. Kindly be sure they are returned to me, however; preferably in one piece."

"Of course," Elizabeth assured him. "It really was a pity she annoyed you when she was making such an effort today to please you."

"To please me?"

"Why, yes, of course. And she didn't think you had even noticed. You really must try to make encouraging comments when she tries so hard."

Gareth stared at his aunt for a moment. "Aunt Bet, I'm afraid I have no earthly idea what you are talking about."

"Why Jessica's demeanor, of course. When I left she was practicing looking 'primly demure like your Meredith,' as she put it. She assured me that from now on she planned on being the very essence of propriety." Elizabeth laughed lightly as she sorted through the maps, fortunately missing the perplexed look on her nephew's face. "Surely you noticed?" Elizabeth glanced questioningly at him.

"I must admit I did notice her appearance, but I'm afraid—words escaped me," Gareth finally managed dryly, clearly visualizing the provocative sight of Jessica amidst the tangled bedclothes. Sometimes he wondered what really went on in his household when he wasn't around.

Elizabeth didn't notice anything odd about his answer. "Jessica did come up with a most interesting supposition on these robberies. Have you thought—?"

Gareth sighed and interrupted her. "Aunt Bet, I don't wish to be rude, but I must finish going over these tariffs as Martindale and the others will arrive momentarily."

"Oh, tonight's your dinner with the other lords. I had quite forgotten. I'll dine upstairs with Jessica then, so you and your friends may discuss politics to your heart's content." She smiled blithely on leaving with the charts.

Gareth shook his head resignedly as he went over to straighten the remaining maps and close the cabinet his aunt had left ajar. He hesitated on noticing the charts she had taken were mostly seacoast rather than inland. That meant she would probably be back when she discovered her error. He ran his hand distractedly through his hair. What he wouldn't give for a few quiet months at Cantonley.

Jessica repaired quickly from her chill, and by the fourth day Elizabeth gave up trying to confine her.

"I believe you are well enough to accompany me to Charlotte Camden's musicale this afternoon," she told an ecstatic Jessica. "I acknowledged the invitation some time ago, before you arrived, but I am certain she would not mind my bringing a guest."

Earlier that morning she'd received Gareth's permission to take the child out, explaining about the musicale. "I'm really surprised we haven't received more invitations for Jessica," Elizabeth commented in concern. "I'm afraid all she seemed to meet at Meredith's ball were those of the young officer group, and of course, having to leave early like that, I suppose the other young ladies just didn't get to know her well. Perhaps you could have Meredith speak to her friends and ask that they include Jessica in future invitations."

Gareth reluctantly agreed to approach Meredith. Actually he had rather avoided her the last few days, merely having his secretary, Thomas, arrange for the requisite flowers to be sent after the ball with a note expressing his pleasure. He too had been surprised that none of the gentry had called on Jessica, especially since the garrison officers obviously found her quite acceptable. However, as Gareth had no close friends with children her age whom he could question, he'd let the matter pass. Launching a young female was not something he was especially adept at anyway, he rationalized. He wasn't overly concerned about her future, as he was still being harassed daily by young officers. Gareth realized he should allow her to begin seeing them. Jessica wasn't particularly class-conscious, and finding a young man she liked, would probably be quite content marrying a soldier. The thought of her in the garrison life, however, caused Gareth such annoyance that he again curtly dismissed the next young hopeful to come by, even though Jessica was well up to receiving callers.

After Jessica and Elizabeth left for the musicale, Gareth had his phaeton brought about, having philosophically decided he owed Meredith a visit. Earlier that day he had sent her his card, inviting her for a ride in the park. He knew she wouldn't be going to the musicale, as it was being given by one of the county baronet's daughters, who Meredith would doubtless consider beneath her notice.

Meredith represented the ultimate in young womanhood as she curtsied charmingly to the earl. "My lord, I was beginning to fear you had forgotten me." She smiled so sweetly that the green-eyed child who had been teasing at the corners of Gareth's mind all morning was supplanted.

"How could I forget such loveliness? My dear, today you exceed even yourself," he said truthfully. On impulse he turned the proffered hand and kissed her sensitive palm. The reaction he read in her eyes brought to mind the intensity of her response to his kisses and he frowned slightly as he led her out to where his groom waited with the high perch phaeton. Were he actually able to believe her passion was indicative of her love for him, he would have welcomed it. However, he well knew, had there been personable gentlemen with greater wealth and title about, her feelings would quickly waver.

As they drove through the broad, sun-dappled paths of Regent's Park, Gareth's thoughts mellowed. After all, he should consider himself fortunate to be marrying a woman capable of adult responses. Some of his friends had found that their delicately raised wives actually considered the marital bed a distasteful duty. All too often in such instances, the wives were soon relegated to the breeding of heirs and serving as hostess to the man's estate, while elsewhere a mistress tended to his other needs. This was definitely not the type of marriage the earl wished for.

Gareth glanced down at the woman at his side. Perhaps he was being foolish to let her responses worry him. He would just have to make certain no other man dared approach her.

"Is your father presently at home?" Gareth asked after a while, having determined it was time to go ahead with the matter of their nuptials.

"Oh dear, I'm afraid he is off at my brother's farm in Kent." Meredith fumed inwardly at such bad luck. Here Gareth finally planned to discuss a date for their wedding, and her father had to be off helping that bumpkin George with some silly problem again! "He should be back by tomorrow noon, I'm sure," she added hopefully.

"I'm afraid tomorrow is a rather important session in the House of Lords, but perhaps I will see him there if he returns in time to attend."

"I'm sure he will, if possible." Meredith made a mental note to insist her father go to the parliamentary meeting the next day whether he wanted to or not. "What is of such importance?" she asked innocently.

The earl's mind, however, had already wandered to the House of Lords meeting and he misinterpreted the question. "We are considering some new tariffs. It might be a rather heavy addition to the taxing system, but I believe it would improve the general roads and provide better facilities for townships. I personally think it quite worthwhile, however the younger set of landowners is giving us considerable opposition so we shall need all the votes—"

"Gareth!" Meredith interrupted him rudely. "Whatever are you talking about?" She couldn't manage to keep the irritation from her voice. What was he thinking? Going on about this—this tariff nonsense, when they were discussing their wedding! At Gareth's annoyed glance, Meredith quickly changed her tone. "Gareth, I do beg your pardon, but you know I'm totally lost in those male subjects." She pouted temptingly. "It's such a beautiful day, couldn't we stop for a few minutes and just walk down the paths, then perhaps you can explain some of these tariffs to me?" She smiled, confident that with another kiss she would bring his lordship's mind back to really important matters.

Gareth frowned, but obligingly drew up his bays. "As a matter of fact, there is something else I wished to discuss with you," he said, remembering his aunt's request on Jessica's behalf.

Meredith smiled smugly, gesturing for the groom to wait with the carriage as he handed her down. But her hopes were soon dashed again when he brought up Jessica's name.

That stupid girl was certainly taking up too much of his thoughts! But at least she didn't have to worry about her as competition. What any man would want with the red-haired minx was anyone's guess, Meredith thought in exasperation as she half listened to Gareth. The memory of Gareth enjoying himself dancing with the little witch still galled her. But after what she had discovered from Caroline Marcotte, she knew neither Gareth nor any other of the gentry would be having anything to do with Miss McDowell.

It hadn't been until after Gareth left her ball early that Meredith joined the group of her close friends. She had found them gossiping even more avidly than usual, and was quickly delighted with the subject.

Anne Marcotte, Caroline's mother and the former Anne Westley, had somehow gotten wind of the Earl of Cantonley returning from settling a Scottish laird's estate and bringing some young female relative back in his protection. Anne knew the story being circulated was that Jessica was Laird McDowell's niece, but also knew that it could not be the truth.

Since Anne had been engaged to the laird's son, Robert, she knew the family well. Robert's only uncle was much too old to have sired a daughter Jessica's age, besides which, Anne was sure she knew who this girl really was.

Years ago she had heard through the mysterious grapevine of servants' chatter, that Robert, her fiancé, had indeed sired a child with some Irish woman, and worse, that the laird was actually supporting the child. Even after Robert's death and herself comfortably married, it still chafed her that Robert had been seeing some strumpet while engaged to her. There had even been rumors that he had wanted to call off their own marriage because of that hussy!

Anne had almost been relieved that Robert had died and spared her such shame. She had never even considered forgiving him.

Gareth had not been aware of her presence in the crowded rooms of Meredith's ball, which was the way Anne had planned it. She had wanted to get a glimpse of the girl, and when she had, she was certain. Seeing Jessica, she easily recognized Robert's gentle features, and all her fury at his betrayal came back to the surface.

Anne had long been awed by the quiet, intelligent son of her father's friend. The Westleys had a small property near the laird in Scotland, where they often spent their summers. Robert was always kind to the Westleys' rather plain daughter, treating her much as a sister through their summers together. He never realized the families' interpretation of his attention to the girl, nor her feelings for him. When they reached marriageable age, everyone simply took it for granted that the two of them would wed.

At that time Robert hadn't known many other females, being more involved in his studies than socializing. He truly liked Anne and didn't wish to hurt either her or their parents, who also wished the union. Not too interested in marriage at all, Robert decided Anne would make as good a wife as any, and asked for her hand.

They probably would have managed fine together, except unfortunately only a few months before the wedding date, Robert went on a botanical trip to Ireland, and there discovered what love really was.

"So I thought perhaps you might invite Jessica on outings with your group of friends, as she doesn't know many young people," Gareth finished. Meredith hadn't heard most of what he'd said since she'd smugly been planning her own announcement.

"Gareth, I am so terribly sorry to be the one to have to tell you this," Meredith told him in distress, "but I'm afraid that is impossible, as we all know about Jessica's—well, lineage."

Gareth listened in stony silence as Meredith related what her friend Caroline Marcotte had told her. "Anne Marcotte, Caroline's mother, was engaged to Robert McDowell, and

Lady Marcotte is quite certain this girl is his—his child." Meredith looked away in feigned embarrassment. "And Robert, of course, was never married, so I'm sure you understand there is no way anyone of *our* set could possibly associate with her." She gestured helplessly. "I do feel sorry for the girl, but we were all more upset at the possibility you had been taken in by her and her solicitor like that. Of course, everyone recognized that it was hardly your fault," she volunteered.

Gareth held his fury at a slow boil.

"Surely you knew about this by now?" Meredith added uneasily. Her parents had told her she was definitely not to mention anything of her discovery to anyone. "Not that it should be our concern, but we all thought that you were just waiting until Jessica recovered from her illness before making some other arrangements for her keep."

"Doubtless Caroline and your other *friends* have spread this story all over town?" Gareth inquired coldly, suddenly remembering he'd allowed Elizabeth to take Jessica to the musicale.

"Gareth, you know how the *ton* is. We couldn't just stand by and let our friends commit a social blunder such as associating with a—" She stopped at his look, then hurried on to explain. "Of course, with *your* status, no one would dare say anything about your association with her, but for instance, Philip, Viscount Loursine's son, had actually intended approaching you to call on her!" Meredith was quite certain he would understand.

"I assume you set young Philip straight?" Gareth's voice was almost casual.

"Naturally. Can you imagine how mortified he would have been? Philip had to leave early from my ball and had not spoken to any of us who knew about her. He was, I believe, rather taken by Jessica's Irish looks." She laughed at the thought. "Those garrison officers were certainly interested in her," she offered consideringly. "You know, as they can seldom expect to marry into real society, perhaps one of them might overlook her lineage." Meredith was certain Gareth's annoyance could be attributed to his concern for getting rid of the girl. "A pity of course. I suppose since this is known, she will certainly not inherit from the Scottish estate. That would have at least provided some dowry to encourage a suitor." Meredith and her friends had all been quite curious as to whether the earl would contest handing over the laird's estate to some illegitimate brat.

Gareth easily saw through her query. "You and your friends can rest assured that Jessica will have an exceedingly generous dowry," he snapped coldly, "as I will be responsible for it."

Meredith was shocked into momentary silence as he led her back to the phaeton in icy silence.

"Gareth, what are you doing?" she exclaimed impatiently, realizing he had headed the carriage back to her own street.

"Returning you to your mother," he said curtly, "as I must go see how badly your gossiping with your friends has harmed Jessica."

She glared at him. "What are you talking about? My friends and I have done nothing but learn the truth about that—" At his look she turned away with a haughty sniff and rode in disdainful silence for the remainder of the short trip.

Lady Summerwood and her friend Lady Crompton were just exiting the Summerwood home on their way to the lending library, when the earl's carriage tooled about the corner.

"Why, isn't that Lord St. John?" Lady Crompton questioned. "I thought you said Meredith had just driven out to the park with him?"

"She did. I cannot imagine why they have returned

already," Lady Summerwood said curiously as the earl pulled his horses to a halt.

"Why, dear"—Lady Summerwood moved forward anxiously as Gareth coldly handed Meredith down from the carriage—"you are back so soon. Is something wrong?" At seeing her daughter's flushed face, she turned to Gareth, her alarm growing at his stony expression.

"My apologies, Lady Summerwood," Gareth offered, "but I have had to change our plans as a family matter has come to my attention that I must attend to immediately."

"Family," Meredith scoffed, her fury at his daring to ignore her pouting for the whole trip overcoming her better judgment. "Jessica is not any real kin to you. And I will have you know I do not appreciate being placed second to some little nobody."

"Meredith"—the earl's tone gave grim warning—"Jessica is my ward and I care for her well-being."

"Meredith, please now, dear." Her mother frantically tried to ward off the disaster she saw brewing, but the girl unwisely chose to ignore her.

"You care about Jessica? And what of me? I am your fiancée—you should be more concerned about my well-being than that of Jessica."

The earl, carefully containing his emotions, merely gave her a silent look before addressing her mother. "Lady Summerwood, if you would see your daughter inside?"

As he turned to his equipage, Meredith stomped her foot in fury. "Don't you dare turn your back on me, Lord St. John!"

The earl stopped.

"You are quite overwrought now, dear." Her mother again tried unsuccessfully to intervene as her friend gaped at the melodrama. "Why don't we just go inside and—"

"No, Mother. I will not be treated like this." Meredith glared at the earl. "If you are so concerned about that stupid girl, perhaps you should be marrying her instead of me." She ripped the St. John emerald from her hand and flung it to the grass at his feet before running into the house.

"Lord St. John." Lady Summerwood rushed forward. "Meredith is only upset. She really doesn't mean—"

"I believe Miss Summerwood made her meaning quite clear," the earl said coldly, picking up the ring and dropping it into his vest pocket.

"No, no. I am quite sure once she—"

"Good day, Lady Summerwood. Madam." He nodded brusquely to Lady Crompton before climbing onto the phaeton.

Lady Crompton and the footman rushed to Lady Summerwood as she swayed weakly.

"Oh, good heavens! Now see what that foolish girl has done." Lady Summerwood willingly accepted the footman's help back to the house.

Chapter Five

"Aunt Bet, I particularly owe you an apology for not being truthful concerning Jessica's parentage," Gareth added, after explaining what had happened. "You mustn't blame Jessica either, as I told her to go along with the story of her being the laird's niece, rather than granddaughter."

"Gareth, I do understand, but surely you should have known you could trust me." Elizabeth sighed. "But that doesn't really matter. The question is: how shall we stop these awful rumors?"

Gareth turned to Jessica. "This is exactly the kind of situation I had hoped to shield you from." Jessica had been sitting in almost stunned silence as Elizabeth told how the baronet's servants had actually barred her from the manor when they arrived. "I was naive to think the matter could be concealed," Gareth continued, "but with your parentage being Irish, I had hoped the London *ton* would not find out."

"It is all right, Your Lordship," Jessica finally said in a

quiet voice. "I should never have come back here with you. I am terribly sorry to have caused you and Aunt Bet such embarrassment. I—I suppose I never realized what it meant that my parents were not—" Her voice broke as silent tears ran down her cheeks.

Gareth cursed at the baronet's family under his breath as he went over to Jessica. "Listen, child, what your parents did or failed to do is no fault of yours. They loved each other and planned to marry had your father not died." He used her own words, whether true or not, hoping they would make her feel better. "You have nothing to apologize to anyone for. It is rather I who should apologize to you for exposing you to this situation."

"Sir, you haven't—"

Gareth stopped her protest. "The past cannot be changed; however, you needn't concern yourself further with any of this. I shall take care of matters. Now you go up to your room and wash away those tears. Aunt Bet will join you shortly." He gently guided her out.

When Jessica left, he turned to Elizabeth. "Aunt, we will be moving to Cantonley in the morning. If you will, please have the servants begin preparation immediately."

"Cantonley?" She looked at him in shock. "Surely you are not serious, Gareth. This is the middle of the season. Whatever will Meredith say?"

"Damn Meredith!" Gareth saw Elizabeth's eyes widen. "I beg your pardon, Aunt Bet, but it was Meredith and her friends who spread this tale all over London. And I had actually intended on speaking with her father tomorrow to set a date for the wedding," he added bitterly.

"You—are you saying you are *not* going to wed Meredith?" Elizabeth asked in amazement.

"Correct, I am not going to marry Meredith," he answered shortly. "Perhaps you should go and check on Jessica. She is understandably upset."

Elizabeth looked at her nephew in concern but knew better than to press him further in his current mood.

After his aunt left, Gareth went to his desk and penned a short note to Meredith and her parents. He explained that for the good of his young relative Jessica, it was necessary that his household remove themselves to his country estate. As he doubtless would not be back except on business, he was regretfully canceling all future social engagements in London for the remainder of the season. That would suffice to inform Meredith and her parents that he was no longer in contention for her hand. He folded the note and decisively sealed the wax with his signet ring. Even though still furious, Gareth felt a great weight lifted from his mind as he rang for his secretary.

"Thomas, have this delivered to the Summerwood residence in the morning and kindly go through my calendar and send regrets on any appointments for the rest of the season, other than the House of Lords, of course. I will come back into town for most of those meetings."

"Back in town, sir?"

"Yes, I'm moving the family to Cantonley, though I would appreciate it if you would remain here with some staff to keep this residence open. I will be back and forth on parliamentary business for the next month or so, after which you may join us at the estate."

The earl wrote a few more personal notes to friends before proceeding upstairs to check on Jessica and Elizabeth. He disliked having to remove Elizabeth from London in the midst of the season like this, as he knew she enjoyed the activities. Most of the families from the country would also be in town now, leaving little social life for the family at Cantonley. Personally, however, he was not displeased at having a good excuse to escape the *ton*.

Jessica rose hesitantly from before the fire when the earl entered her room.

"Where is Aunt Bet?" Gareth had expected to find them together.

"She had to go to the kitchen. Cook was having a problem with some tradesman," Jessica replied, then continued anxiously, "but could I—speak to you, my lord?"

Gareth gestured for her to take her seat and took the other chair himself. "Jessica, I realize how upsetting this is, but I assure you that you shall never again be subjected to such embarrassments as you were today. There is no need for you to concern yourself further. I wish you to simply forget the entire matter."

"Thank you, but it is not just that, my lord. Aunt Bet said you're removing the household to your country estate?"

"Yes, I think that will be best under the circumstances. It will take you from the reach of the gossipmongers until the matter runs it course, as it surely will. Such tales are quickly forgotten whenever the *ton* finds something else to titter about," he said lightly, hoping to soothe her.

"Oh, sir." Jessica stood up in agitation. "I really—I just cannot allow you to go to all of this trouble on my behalf!"

"Allow me?" Gareth raised a brow mockingly. "I'm afraid, brat, that the ordering of my affairs is not in your hands."

Jessica smiled weakly. "Please, Your Lordship, I have caused you nothing but problems from first we met. You and Aunt Bet cannot forgo the whole season just for me. I can—"

"Jessica," he interrupted, rising and leading her firmly back to her chair, "to be quite honest, I have for some time been more than ready to retire back to my estate. Normally, I never stay in London more than a few weeks of the season, as I find the constant social obligations tedious. This year I have only remained this long because of—very personal considerations."

Jessica mistook his frown as he thought of Meredith.

"Your Lordship, you are affianced to Meredith," she protested. "You cannot want to be away from her for so long. I truly would not mind staying at your estate, if you so wish. There is no need for both you and Aunt Bet to—"

"I am no longer engaged to Miss Summerwood."

Jessica looked up in dismay, misunderstanding the bitterness in his voice.

"Oh, sir! Surely that stupid girl did not turn you down because of—of your kinship to me! Please," she said frantically, "you can tell her family it was all a preposterous lie. Like you thought at first. Tell them I had convinced you I was really the laird's legitimate granddaughter. We can say that—you've discovered the whole thing was an absurd ruse. That I was just after the laird's estate after all. They really want to believe that anyway. Then I will be of no kin to you and—"

Jessica was startled from her elaborate planning, as Gareth burst into laughter. "My dear Jessica, I truly appreciate your generous offer, but I scarcely believe this plan is necessary. I no longer wish to wed Meredith."

"But—why?" She looked at him in confusion. "You were going to marry her, you told me that. So you must love her."

"Love her?" Gareth hesitated, finding himself oddly reluctant to admit his much less than noble reasons for selecting Meredith as his countess. "I'm afraid that you shall find that in society, marriages are often based on reasons other than love."

"I know," she said. "Aunt Bet told me some are for properties and titles and such, but you already have those things. *You* surely would not marry someone you didn't love!"

Gareth silently looked at her a moment before deciding the subject was better changed. "I must ask your help with Aunt Bet, Jessica." He knew that would gain her attention.

"Although I am well ready to go back to Cantonley, Elizabeth is quite another matter. She enjoys the social season, so I must depend on you to come up with some diversions. Aunt Bet is pleased with your company. I am sure the two of you can contrive some interesting things to do. Later on, perhaps we can manage to arrange a late season at Bath," he offered, giving her matters other than her own problems to think about.

The following morning, Gareth send ahead Jessica, Elizabeth, and the numerous carriages of the entourage necessary to move the household on to Cantonley. He planned on meeting them at an inn halfway to the estate that evening after completing some additional business in town.

Once on the road, Elizabeth realized Jessica was still distraught over having made the move necessary, and sought to distract her by bringing up the subject of the highwaymen. Elizabeth had brought the maps and now spread them out. "Look, Jessica, we'll be traveling that very road where those robberies of yours took place." She traced their route with her finger. Elizabeth secretly found the possibility of actually seeing the outlaws rather exciting. But then, realizing such a prospect might alarm a young girl, added, "Of course, Gareth has assigned armed outriders to accompany us, so there is little chance the highwaymen would risk coming near."

"You don't suppose?" Jessica sounded so disappointed that Elizabeth gave her a surprised look, but Jessica continued before she could comment. "The robberies were right along in here, were they not?" Jessica pointed to a section of the map. "Will we be passing through that area?"

"Hmm, yes. That bridge there is, in fact, the beginning of Cantonley lands. If this good weather lasts, we should reach that stretch by mid-morning tomorrow."

"Really? Why one of the robberies took place on a

bridge!" Jessica said excitedly, and Elizabeth knowing full well what she was thinking, laughed.

"Oh, dear. Gareth would frown upon your hope to meet up with the robbers!"

"Oh, I wasn't—" Jessica began. "Well, I've never seen real bandits, and these haven't actually hurt anyone. After all, they are dubbed 'gentlemen bandits,' and according to the articles they are described as being quite young and handsome!"

"You can just put those notions out of your mind, miss," Elizabeth forced herself to say sternly. "Highwaymen are not proper at all, gentlemen or no."

"Oh, I suppose," Jessica admitted begrudgingly, "though would it not be exciting to find some solution to this mystery for His Lordship? If only we could just discover whether the highwaymen really are escaping to the sea."

"Well, let's see." Elizabeth's own sense of adventure took hold and she leaned over to study the map. "Baker's Inlet does seem like such a likely spot, and it is quite close to the manor. We could perhaps—" She stopped herself. "Whatever am I thinking? Gareth would simply have apoplexy."

"No, that is an excellent thought." Jessica latched on to the possibilities, waving off the earl's likely concern. "We could just go over alone to see if there are any signs of a ship; no one need even know. Surely Lord St. John keeps riding horses, does he not?"

"Yes, actually I'm afraid that is just what I was thinking." Elizabeth easily gave up her scruples in sight of adventure. "There is even a riding trail along the shoreline here, but I've never ridden beyond, let's see, this field." She pointed to a square area on the map. "Gareth generally has it planted in fodder grains. Oh, this is going to be so much more exciting than some silly London season!"

* * *

His lordship, the earl, happily unaware what the ladies of his household planned, was at that moment preparing to leave London when he was stopped by someone hailing him.

"Y'er Lordship. Beggin' y'er pardon, milord, but could I 'ave a word with you?"

Gareth glanced around to find Angus Conners, one of the men who grew up on Cantonley, approaching him. The earl dismounted from the leggy roan, a new acquisition he'd planned to try out on the cross-country ride to the inn.

"Of course, Angus. You just caught me. I was setting out for Cantonley, in fact. What has you up in these parts?"

"Livin' 'ere now, we are. The wife and me," Angus declared proudly. "Got on with the Runners, I did. Was mostly Y'er Lordship's kind voucher what did it, I might add. I've been 'oping for a chance to give my thanks. 'Ad to be in person, as I don't write so well."

Gareth smiled, clapping the man on the shoulder. He had almost forgotten writing the letter recommending Angus to the Bow Street Runners. "Well, they couldn't have found a better man. I am pleased to have been able to help."

"As it 'appens, I'm soon off back to Cantonley. Been assigned to those robbers on y'er own lands, sir. They figured as I was raised there and all, I'd know the lay of things. So me partner and me will be needin' a permission letter from y'er agent to ride the property, if you'd oblige."

"Of course. I'm pleased to have you on the job. My sheriff over there hasn't had much luck against that pair. I'm glad he called in Bow Street. Come on in and I'll have Thomas prepare you a letter now. Will you be heading down there immediately?" Gareth asked as he escorted the other man into the house.

"Not myself, for a sen'night, though Ben, he's my

partner, will be 'eading out first 'o the week. I'm sailin' to Dublin on the morrow to 'elp bring a prisoner back."

"Dublin?" Gareth had a thought. "Are you going to have much time there?"

"Couple of days, mostly just awaitin' the proper writs." Angus looked curiously at the earl. "Somethin' you'd be needin' up there, sir?"

"Yes, as a matter of fact. There just might be," Gareth said consideringly as he rang for Thomas.

Gareth was not unduly surprised to find both ladies back in high spirits that night when he escorted them into the inn's private parlor for dinner. One of the aspects that had always made Elizabeth his favorite relative was her infinite good temper. Jessica, he had quickly discovered, had the same quality. Quite the opposite from Meredith, he thought irrelevantly. He had known her to pout for days when he had been forced to break some appointment. He found himself more and more relieved to be finished with that one, despite her outward loveliness.

Thinking of beauty, he glanced over at Jessica. She was wearing one of her new gowns with pale yellow satin stripes that lent her an almost ethereal air. "I gather the trip has not been too arduous, as the both of you seem in good spirits?" Gareth inquired politely as he assumed his own seat after settling the ladies. "Have you thought of some interesting diversions to engage in at Cantonley?"

"Oh, yes. We've planned a number of things to occupy us, haven't we, dear?" Elizabeth assured him, giving Jessica a warning glance.

"Yes, a number," Jessica agreed demurely, and for no reason he could quite discern, Gareth began to get an uneasy feeling.

"Very good." He studied the pair a moment. "And, what

are some of these plans?" he inquired purposefully of Jessica.

"Oh, um." Jessica looked at Elizabeth in panic. "Painting. That's what," she said happily. "We shall do sketches of the shorebirds."

"Yes, watercolors," Elizabeth added quickly, on seeing Gareth's eyes narrow in suspicion. "Jessica has said she is adept with paints and shall show me. It is something I've always wanted to learn."

"Hmm. That sounds pleasant enough." Gareth nodded, still somehow dubious. Why were the ladies of his household acting so nervous? "What else have you planned?"

"Else?" both women chimed. "Well, riding naturally." Elizabeth filled the awkward moment of silence. "Cantonley has such lovely bridle trails. I'm quite looking forward to showing Jessica, and you know how I love the outdoors."

"Yes. Riding, definitely," Jessica agreed a bit too brightly, but Gareth was diverted as the innkeeper and his young son came in with well-laden trays.

Gareth couldn't help but be amused as the young lad tried very obviously to keep his eyes off the flame-haired young lady as he served the table, but almost of their own volition, his eyes kept wandering to Jessica. Jessica didn't make matters easier for him, as she smiled up sweetly in thanks when the lad placed her plate before her, causing his face to instantly turn scarlet.

As soon as the pair departed, Elizabeth quickly entered into a long, amusing account of some riding incident from her youth. She said mention of the riding trails had brought it to mind, her true intention, however, being to distract Gareth from his previous line of questioning.

Gareth listened with enjoyment to the story, but suspected that it was mostly contrived. "Aunt Bet," he said, laughing at the end, "why have you never told this incident before? I thought I had heard all of your anecdotes."

"I do believe I had totally forgotten about it. I was just a green girl when that happened, much as Jessica now," she said lightly.

"Green girl?" Jessica sniffed at this presumed put-down. "Aunt Bet, I am almost eighteen. That is scarcely a girl."

Gareth and Elizabeth both chuckled at her indignation. "Almost eighteen? I thought you were barely seventeen," the earl teased.

"I shall be eighteen before the year is out."

"December fifteenth, didn't you say, dear?" Elizabeth reminded her gently.

"Which I believe is yet over half a year away," Gareth added.

"Well, perhaps, but scarcely a green girl! Wherever do people come up with such peculiar descriptions anyway? Why should they call any girl 'green'?"

Gareth laughed. "I believe the term came from fruits or vegetables that are green when immature or unripe."

"Well." Jessica drew up in a huff, her dignity affronted by the two of them laughing at her. "I shouldn't consider myself 'unripe'!"

Unfortunately at that very moment the innkeeper's son was re-entering with a heavy tea tray. At her words, his eyes flew immediately to her revealing décolletage, and the tray began to clatter perilously.

"Oh, dear, let me help." Jessica jumped up and steadied the tray. Her proximity, however, was more than the flustered boy could take. With a horrified glance at the earl, he shoved the tray into her keeping, and without so much as a word, fled the room.

Gareth tried to school his features, but gave up as Elizabeth erupted into helpless peals of laughter, mopping her face with her napkin. "Oh my, I do begin to see what you have been through, Gareth," she said as the grinning earl retrieved the tray from Jessica.

"Whatever do you two find so amusing?" Jessica fumed. "I was trying to help that silly boy and he practically threw the tray at me! I really think you should speak to him, Your Lordship," she decreed.

"I probably should reassure the poor lad." Gareth chuckled. "He is no doubt expecting to be horsewhipped for insubordination. However, under the circumstances, I believe he behaved most commendably."

"Commendably, indeed? Whatever are you talking about? What circumstances?" Jesse demanded.

"Here, child." Elizabeth finally regained control and soothed her. "Sit down and finish your meal. The boy, I fear, was just a bit flustered by your presence."

"Well I can't imagine what there is about me to cause anyone to become flustered, much less to fling a tray at me!"

The meal had finally resumed some semblance of normalcy when the innkeeper hurried back into the room. "Milord, I just seen my son flee from here as if someone was chasing him. I do pray he's done nothing to cause your displeasure?"

The earl rose and ushered the man back out, reassuring him. "It was nothing. I'm afraid my ward turned and—unsettled the tray as the boy brought it," he said to save the boy a thrashing. "It wasn't his fault, but I fear he expected we'd be angry. Actually no harm was done, so please reassure the lad that he has nothing to worry about. The meal is quite superior," he added by way of distracting the man.

The remainder of their dinner was completed in relative harmony with no more untoward incidents. The diversions distracted the earl from his earlier suspicions, and the ladies were pleased that the conversation never returned to their plans at Cantonley.

Both Elizabeth and Jessica were rather disappointed the

next day when no robbers appeared on the final leg of their journey, though Jessica was delighted as they entered the outskirts of Cantonley land and the road began to border the seashore. She had never seen the ocean and tried in vain to get Elizabeth to have the carriage stop.

Elizabeth just laughed. "But my dear, we'll arrive at the manor in just a bit over half an hour, and Cantonley has its own beach—much nicer than these. You really must be patient."

There was a good half mile of meticulously landscaped roadway heralding the earldom of Cantonley even before the massive stone gatehouse appeared. Jessica was amazed. In her limited travels to and from school, she had passed some large estates, but they compared not at all to this one.

An elderly gatekeeper hobbled over quickly from where he'd been tending a rose bed. "Milord," he said in concern as he wrestled with the great hinged gate, "we hadn't had no word you were coming."

"Sorry, William." Gareth gestured to a footman to help swing the unwieldy gates. "It was a sudden decision. I had no time to send a message. I'm going to have to get a metalsmith out—these old gates need to be rehinged," he added to excuse having to seek help for the old man. William had been his father's valet for years and then became butler. He was now too old for almost any duties, but had asked not to be pensioned off. William's wife had died several years before, and he said he had to have something to do to pass the time. The gatekeeper position was an ideal solution as it required very little work. "Are there any of your Beth's daughters needing a position by chance?" Gareth asked, knowing William had six granddaughters who helped out on occasion at the manor.

"Aye. I'm sure there'll be several happy to come out from the village." William peered curiously at the carriage. "You wouldn't be having brought your Miss Summerwood with you?" Typically, all the servants knew his plans, and William was an old enough retainer to take the liberty of asking outright.

Gareth smiled resignedly. "No, but I do have a young lady, Miss Jessica McDowell from Ireland, with us. She will be staying here, as my ward." He hesitated, but then knowing word would get out anyway, continued, "Miss Summerwood and I will not be getting married."

The old man's eyes brightened in interest.

Just then Elizabeth leaned from the carriage window. "William, how good to see you looking well. You were down with your gout, I believe, when we left?" The look she cast Gareth let him know she was helping him escape further questioning. Even from the time they were children, William had always been able to find out everything from them.

"Miss Elizabeth, you're looking fine yourself." The old man came over, having successfully been distracted from his former line of questioning. "My foot's a lot better. That gout, it comes and it goes." He shrugged dismissively. "And this'll be the young lady, Miss Jessica?" He peered into the carriage.

"Yes, sir." Jessica smiled happily back, liking the old man on sight. "I am pleased to meet you," she declared as politely as if she were meeting a lord, when Elizabeth introduced him.

The old man chuckled. "I am right pleased to meet you, too. An Irish lass you be, with all that red hair. Lucky, you know, a red-haired lass." He winked sagely at Gareth. "Make some pretty little freckled-faced babies, too, she would." He merely grinned at Gareth's stern look as he hobbled over to let the carriages pass. "Roses are real fine this time," he called to them. "I'll send you lasses up some in a bit."

"What a delightful old gentleman." Jessica waved to him

as they passed through the gate. "But why ever did he tell His Lordship I should have pretty, freckled children? What a decidedly odd thing to say."

Elizabeth hid a grin. "William does come up with some fanciful ideas, and I'm afraid he takes complete advantage of the fact that we love him too dearly to ever call him down on anything he says, regardless of how outrageous. You shall simply have to get used to him. My, his roses really are lovely—look at those beds over there." She distracted the girl, pointing out some more flowers.

"Oh look, you can see the manor. Why, it's immense, isn't it?" Jessica looked up excitedly as the carriages rounded the last small bend. "Heavens. It's more like a castle!" The manor rose fully into sight across the manicured acres of lawn and shrubbery. Towers stood a story above the three main floors. Indeed it was a castle, albeit an ancient Norman one, from which the original structure had evolved, Elizabeth explained to Jessica.

"Romand, Gareth's ancestor who built the castle, was a Norman duke who settled here when he tired of pirating the coastline. See"—she pointed out a centralized section—"this was apparently an expanded adaptation of the Norman motte-and-bailey castle, which was basically just a mound, a 'motte,' with palisade and tower, surrounded by a ditched and palisaded enclosure, the 'bailey.' Romand later added a second tower to match the first and another story toward the rear you can't see from here. Each successor made additions. The palisades and bailey were displaced by lawns, although Gareth saved some of the original ditch to the rear, through which he has re-routed his trout stream."

The conversation was interrupted as the carriage pulled up before the imposing manor. The earl dismounted and came over to help the ladies out after sending the footmen scrambling to notify the household of their arrival.

"Your Lordship, this is a magnificent home. Aunt Bet

was just telling me a little of its history," Jessica remarked as he handed her down the carriage steps.

"About Romand, no doubt." The earl raised a brow at his aunt. "I do believe that old rogue has long since captured Aunt Bet's fancy. She is a bit of a romantic, I fear. Fortunately, there are no real pirates about or she'd probably set out to catch herself one," he joked before turning to introduce to Jessica the housekeeper and butler who had hurried out.

The inside of the manor had obviously been completely renovated from its ancient beginnings. A checkered marble hallway, open to the second story, graced the entrance. Marble was used likewise for the wide curving stairway ascending to the next level. The upper hallway circling the entry was open except for a sturdy, intricately carved balustrade. Beautifully worked doors led to the rooms on either side of the entranceway. Gareth led them to the first of these, revealing a lovely parlor decorated in burgundy and cream.

"Perhaps you can arrange a tea tray in here for us, Agnes?" he asked the flustered housekeeper. "I am aware we were not expected, but I'm sure Martha must have baked some of those delightful scones today."

Jessica flitted happily about the beautifully appointed room, asking about everything from the bisque figure collection, which had belonged to Gareth's mother, clear down to the wide red oak flooring revealed about the edges of the subtly hued Persian carpet.

"Child, do come and sit down," Elizabeth finally instructed. "I'm sure you must be tired from that long trip."

"Heavens, Aunt Bet, all we've done is sit for hours," Jessica protested, nonetheless choosing a cushioned chair between the two of them.

"I think you have finally met your match for endurance,

Aunt," Gareth chuckled, "but at least I doubt either of you will be bored. Ah, here is Agnes with a tray."

"May I serve?" At Elizabeth's nod, Jessica gracefully executed the almost ritualistic pouring of the tea and served the delicate pastries to the other two, before sitting back with her own.

"You seem to have been taught the social amenities," the earl commented, watching her.

Jessica wrinkled her nose, spoiling the ladylike effect previously established. "What is there to learn? Anyone can pour tea. Speaking of learning though, Aunt Bet mentioned that you have a massive library here, much larger even than in your London house. I should love to see it."

The earl smiled at her obvious hint. "You are welcome to use my library—providing, of course, the scissors are safely out of reach," he added dryly. "However, this evening I have a lot of estate matters to catch up on with my agent and you will be busy getting settled in, so perhaps it can wait until the morning."

As predicted, arranging their rooms and settling their belongings took the remainder of the afternoon. The cook outdid herself with a high tea that afternoon which, after an escorted tour of the whole castle, from the towers to the wine cellar, had both of the ladies content to settle down for an early night.

Jessica arose at daybreak the next morning, eager to begin the day. As Elizabeth preferred to sleep later, Jessica decided to investigate the earl's library while she waited for her friend to arise.

The earl had left the house even earlier to ride the estate with his agent, so Jessica had the library to herself. It was an impressive room, walled in beautiful oak paneling, with two double sets of French doors opening to a stone patio overhanging the beach below.

Jessica immediately went out into the patio to see the

ocean. She'd been firmly forbidden to go down to the beach alone. Both Gareth and Elizabeth had anticipated her immediate desire to wade in the gentle waves, and insisted that one of them or a servant be with her.

Needless to say, Jessica's first thought on looking at the shore was to venture down. Sighing, she forced herself to return to the library. She decided she really must do as his lordship said, as she had quite tried his patience enough in their short time together, although she couldn't see what harm it could do to just go and look at the water, perhaps examine some of the interesting things she'd glimpsed in their brief walk yesterday.

Fortunately, before Jessica managed to talk herself into descending the stone stairway, the earl returned from his morning ride.

"You are up early," he said without any particular enthusiasm, having expected to have his library to himself.

Jessica immediately caught the slight edge to his voice. "I never sleep late, but I will come back another time if you'd prefer." She started to leave, but he detained her.

"That is all right, you may remain. However, I do have some paperwork to attend to, so you must look about on your own."

Jessica dubiously watched the earl as he ignored her and went to his desk at one end of the long room. Finally, with a mental shrug, she walked over to the nearest shelves and soon lost herself in the fascinating array of titles.

Gareth had quite forgotten Jessica was there when sometime later he rose and went to the bell pull to summon a servant to bring a tea tray. He then noticed her curled contentedly on the settee, obviously engrossed in the book on her lap. He studied her in some amazement. In curiosity, he walked over to see what she was reading.

Gareth was slightly taken aback by the girl's annoyed glance as his shadow fell over her page. "Oh, Your

Lordship," she said when she realized who had walked up. "I was so involved trying to translate this French history, I had forgotten you were here," she admitted candidly. "I never realized my French vocabulary was so limited. I keep running across words I don't know at all. Would you perhaps have a French/English dictionary?"

Gareth fetched the requested volume from a separate area of language dictionaries. "You were certainly engrossed," he said wryly. "As a matter of fact, you were so quiet, I had forgotten you were here as well. Was there a particular word you needed?" he asked, flipping open the dictionary as he walked back. He stopped before her in disbelief as she carefully pronounced a word with an explicitly sexual meaning.

Gareth slammed the dictionary shut and snatched the book from her hands, appalled to find it one by a very risqué author. "Of all the books in this library, exactly how did you happen to choose this one?"

Jessica looked up in concern. "You did say I might read any of your books."

"Not this one!"

"Whatever is wrong with that one?" Jessica asked perplexed. "I mentioned I particularly liked history. That is a French version of Queen Mary's reign."

Gareth glanced at the title and stifled a grin. Indeed, *The Reign of Red Marye* could easily be construed as such by an innocent. He glanced through the first pages and was relieved to find the story began when "Marye" was quite young. Jessica had doubtless become bogged down as the author warmed to his subject. "No, this is not a history, but a work of fiction and not at all proper reading for a young lady."

"But I like novels also," Jessica protested, only to be given a quelling glance by Gareth as he placed the book on his desk to be locked away somewhere later. He would definitely have to go through his novels and remove any others of a like nature.

"What else have you selected?" He glanced carefully through the other books beside her.

"I thought, if you don't mind, I would take those poetry volumes to my room to read later." She indicated two of the books. "Actually, I started reading this book by William Gilbert, *De Magnete Magneticisque*, but I got rather lost. I was going to come back to it when I could ask you about some of his concepts, but I didn't want to bother you while you were busy."

Gareth looked at the book incredulously. "You studied this type of science in this school you went to?"

"No, not in any depth. Miss Sophia and Miss Liz didn't see any particular value in magnetism or Gilbert's ideas on astronomy, though we covered the basics on him as well as other scientists. But I have always wanted to find a whole book of his ideas."

"Hmm." The earl had an interest in physics, but couldn't imagine this girl had the capacity to really understand much of Gilbert. "What was it you intended asking me?"

"Oh, primarily just where to find something. All we had at the school were a few science books with bits and pieces on physics. I was so pleased to find a complete book of Gilbert's, but this doesn't seem to explain the basic things. As here"—she opened the book and showed the earl a section—"though Gilbert writes of lodestones and magnets, he doesn't really explain much about them."

"Well, lodestones are just a particular type of rock with a high content of iron ore that allows them to become magnetic," Gareth explained.

"Oh, I know that," Jessica said impatiently. "But what I want to know is why. Why do magnets draw together at opposite poles and repel from the equal? Exactly what is the force that is acting on them? I am certain that it is somewhere in this book, but I could not seem to locate it."

Gareth chuckled. "I am afraid you give Gilbert too much credit. Actually no one, at least to my knowledge, knows exactly what the force is. They have only defined it by its discernible effects and physical properties. Gilbert, however, does go along with Aristotle, Heraclitus, and some of the other ancients in their idea of the animation of the universe." In his enthusiasm for the subject, Gareth forgot his assumption that Jessica wouldn't understand. "This animation, which is magnetism, they likened to being the 'soul' of inanimate objects."

"Yes," Jessica said excitedly, "I once saw a section of Aristotle's 'On the Soul,' where he wrote about the 'animate Mother Earth' and called the lodestone her 'beloved offspring.'"

"I have that book." Gareth went over and pulled several other volumes from the shelves. Gesturing Jessica to the settee, he spread the books about them. "I believe the ancients were identifying magnetism as the life-giving force or energy by comparing it to a 'soul' . . ."

Knowing Jessica's propensity for mischief, it was with some concern that Elizabeth searched for her later on.

"I believe the young miss is in the library, Lady Trenton," the housekeeper said. "At least she was an hour or so ago when I took tea in to His Lordship."

"Oh dear, I do hope she's not bothering Gareth." Elizabeth hurried down the hall only to stop in disbelief at the scene offered as she opened the library door.

Jessica was sitting on the floor before Gareth, actually leaning on his knee as she excitedly pointed out something he was sketching. The two of them were surrounded and partially covered by a jumble of books and papers. They were having such an involved discussion that neither noticed her entrance.

"Whatever are you two doing?" Elizabeth asked in amazement.

"Aunt Bet." Jessica looked up guiltily. "I am sorry. I forgot I had promised to come to your room and wake you at ten."

"At ten o'clock! Good lord!" Gareth pulled out his pocket watch. "I was supposed to meet Lancaster at half past the hour. Here, Jessica, we must finish this later."

Elizabeth stared in disbelief as Gareth casually handed the papers he was sketching to Jessica and hurriedly strode out.

"Oh." Jessica sighed in disappointment. "And we were just getting into Pliny."

Elizabeth sat down rather weakly as she watched the door close behind the earl. She had never known her punctilious nephew to be distracted enough to forget an appointment. "Pliny?" she finally asked, turning to the girl.

"Yes, His Lordship was showing me Pliny's *Rotation of the Spheres*." Jessica caught the bemused expression on Elizabeth's face and misread it. "Don't feel bad. I had never heard of it either, but just look—"

"Please, my dear, not before breakfast," Elizabeth stated firmly, not really having the academic bend of mind the other two seemed to share.

"I did wait on you for breakfast." Jessica arose, shaking out her crumpled skirts. Then, seeing Elizabeth's skeptical glance at the tea remains amongst the books, added hastily, "Except for the tea and scones the housekeeper brought a while ago, but I'm really famished now."

After breakfast, Elizabeth and Jessica decided to go to Baker's Cove to see what they might find. "Today is probably the best time to ride over, since Gareth is going to be at Lancaster's estate all day. He probably hasn't had time to give the stablehands any directions either, such as insisting grooms go with us everywhere," Elizabeth told Jessica.

Later on, cantering down the beach bridle trail, Jessica giggled. "That was quick thinking to tell the stablemaster that we were going over to your friend's house. I thought for certain he was going to make one of the grooms ride with us."

"I know. I'm afraid he anticipated Gareth, even though he hadn't gotten an order. We'll have to be sure to be back on time, though, before Gareth returns."

"Won't His Lordship be angry when he finds out we didn't go to see your neighbor?"

"Well, actually Cecile is in London. I'll just say when we got halfway over there I remembered she wouldn't be at home, so we just rode about the estate."

"Aunt Bet, I fear I am a bad influence on you. Come on, I'll race you to the wood's edge."

The two had been riding for about forty minutes when they approached a small oat field and Elizabeth reined up. "The cove is just beyond that little copse of ash trees over there, so we had best approach quietly."

Jessica nodded, suddenly a little nervous. "Are you sure this isn't dangerous?"

"Of course. You don't think I would lead you into danger, do you?" Elizabeth gave her a hurt look. "Remember, even if we should run across the highwaymen, they haven't hurt anyone, even when they were robbing them. Besides, everyone around here knows Gareth and wouldn't dare accost us."

Jessica didn't argue, but began to have a definite feeling that Aunt Bet was perhaps not what one might consider a very "responsible" adult. But then again, a responsible adult wouldn't be near so much fun.

They made their way carefully around the field. "We

should perhaps lead the horses now," Elizabeth suggested, dismounting, "for added quiet."

The inlet came into view, innocently empty, and the women looked at each other in disappointment. "Well, I guess my idea was wrong," Jessica sighed as they stood surveying the still cove.

"But it seemed like such a logical conclusion. Maybe this isn't the right cove, or maybe they are just off somewhere else right now," Elizabeth suggested.

"Do you know of any other coves?" Jessica asked hopefully.

"Well, no, not really."

"Did you not say a river went back up inland from this one?" Jessica asked, checking the shoreline.

"Yes, right over . . . let me see, it would be that corner there. That dead tree seems to be blocking off the entry."

Jessica looked where she was pointing. "Aunt Bet! That tree has only been down a short while. Notice the leaves. They are only wilted and haven't yet fallen off."

"You mean—"

"Someone has recently cut it, intentionally blocking the view of the river—I'm sure of it! Come on, we can tether the horses here and walk around."

Elizabeth looked dubiously at the marshy ground. "Oh, all right, but these are new boots, so try to stay on higher ground."

Despite their imaginative theories, neither of the two ladies actually expected the sight that met them as they carefully parted the heavy shrubs at the river's edge.

"Oh, my heavens!" Elizabeth exclaimed.

"Shh." Jessica hushed her as they stared at the tall-masted sloop anchored quietly in the mouth of the small river.

"You were right, Jessica, but who would expect such a

beautiful vessel? I'd have thought we should find a rough pirate ship."

"Maurice d'Albrette in a rough pirate's ship? Indeed!"

Both women shrieked as they spun around. Elizabeth lost her footing in the tangled growth and would have fallen had not the distinguished older gentleman behind her caught her arm.

"There, there, ladies. I did not intend to startle you. Are you all right, my dear?" His smile broadened as Elizabeth looked up at him and blushed charmingly.

"Oh, of course. Thank you, sir." She smiled back as Jessica looked on in amazement.

"Aunt Bet!"

"Hmm? Oh, yes. Sir, whatever are you doing on this property?" Somehow the question came out more as a polite inquiry than the intended demand.

"I have a perfect right here," the man said a bit huffily. "I might ask you ladies the same?"

"I beg your pardon?" Elizabeth said haughtily. "These lands belong to my nephew, Gareth St. John, the Earl of Cantonley, sir!"

"Oh." He looked at bit chastened. "The earl's surely not in residence during the season?"

"I am afraid so. But even were he not, I fail to see where that gives you the right to trespass on his property."

"This property belonged to my family long before the earldom even existed." The gentleman frowned. "My Norman relative, Romand, even built the castle that is now Cantonley manor."

"Romand!" Elizabeth's eyes shone. "Jessica, did you hear? This gentleman is kin to Romand, also."

"That is—nice," Jessica murmured unenthusiastically, but neither of the others seemed to notice.

"Also? Yes, I suppose the earl's line is descended from the pirate, though I'd have scarcely thought you would credit it." He looked quizzically at Elizabeth. "You say you are the earl's aunt?"

"Oh, I am sorry. Yes, I am Lady Elizabeth Trenton, Gareth's aunt on his mother's side. This is Miss Jessica McDowell, the earl's ward. And you said you are—I'm afraid I was so startled when you spoke, I have quite forgotten."

"Maurice d'Albrette, Count of Augustine, from the Somme, France, at your service, ladies." He bowed gallantly over Elizabeth's hand with just a quick smile in Jessica's direction.

"A French count and kin to Romand himself," Elizabeth exclaimed. Then added a bit pensively, "Then I suppose of course you are not a pirate?"

He raised his brows questioningly at the disappointment in Elizabeth's tone. "I am afraid not. Though I am avoiding the authorities at the moment, if that would be acceptable? That is actually why I am making use of your delightful cove."

"Avoiding—" Jessica began, but they ignored her.

"Here, this is not a proper place to entertain ladies." The count finally realized they were still standing in the marsh. "If you'll excuse the impropriety, I would be delighted if you ladies would grant me the pleasure of offering you tea aboard my ship. It will be quite proper," he hastened to add, "as my manservant, Ormand, is aboard. In fact, he's probably preparing tea now. And my scoundrel of a nephew should be back momentarily."

"We should be delighted," Elizabeth answered, despite Jessica's withering look. "Come, dear," she chided Jessica, taking the count's arm, "anyone can tell the count is a perfect gentleman."

"Maurice, please, my dear," he said. They smiled happily at each other as he led them over the gangplank that joined his craft to the shore.

Jessica had no idea what to expect aboard the sloop, but it certainly wasn't the table prepared on the open deck, complete with snowy linen and a shining silver tea service.

"I was schooled in England," the count said, explaining his preference for British tea, "and have a number of relatives over here still." He seated the ladies while his stiffly correct servant brought out extra settings as though it were an everyday occurrence for two ladies to appear from the salt marsh to take tea.

"Now, Maurice, you must tell me why ever you are avoiding the authorities."

The gentleman laughed. "You must explain first. Why did I get the definite impression that you are disappointed I am not a pirate? And whatever were you ladies doing out here looking for pirates, anyway? The earl should not allow you out like this without at least a groom!"

Elizabeth looked warningly at Jessica. "We were just exploring. This is not so far from Cantonley by the bridle trails." She bypassed his other questions. "And you said you were related to Romand. He was such a famous pirate I almost hoped you were, too. I must admit, I've looked at his portrait so often and heard stories of his daring exploits so many times, that I've developed quite a *tendre* for the old gentleman."

"A portrait?" In his excitement Maurice forgot his questions about why they were out unchaperoned and looking for pirates. "You actually have a painting of the pirate? I, myself, dearly wanted to go off and try my hand at piracy when I was a youth. But where is this portrait? I should certainly be pleased to see it."

"In the library at Cantonley, but I'm afraid you would be a bit difficult to explain to Gareth—that is, the earl. He is quite friendly, but very—*appropriate*, if you can understand." She smiled. "I fear he would never approve of us having met you here." She sighed. "You know, you actually have some resemblance to Romand."

"Really?" the count asked happily, obviously pleased. "That is one of the reasons I'm here, other than avoiding the law, of course. I'm writing a history about Romand."

"Why are you avoiding the—" Jessica tried to ask again, but Elizabeth cut her off.

"How fabulous. Then you are a writer? Why, we have some of the pirate's papers still in Gareth's library. They're just ship records and the like, but I should think them quite helpful for your research."

"Actual papers! I would love to see them. I have found some from our family's side, but they weren't Romand's own; only some diaries from other relatives." He frowned. "But, until this matter with Daucey can be cleared up, I fear we would be unwelcome in a gentleman's household," he said, sighing.

"Daucey?" Elizabeth questioned.

"Yes. My nephew. He's not really a bad boy, just one of those that seem to tumble into all manner of trouble. I'm afraid I see so much of myself as a youth in him that I find it hard to be too condemning. I had to promise my sister Gwendolyn that I would get him out of the country until they can straighten matters out. This was such an ideal place—out here he could scarcely find any mischief."

He hesitated as though about to elaborate, then thought better of it. "This area is also the perfect atmosphere for my writing, being Romand's actual last home. I determined we could just anchor about here for a few weeks. It was Daucey's idea that we disguise the entrance—he is a bit dramatic."

Elizabeth and Jessica looked at each other. "Your nephew, Daucey, where is he now?" Elizabeth finally asked.

"Oh, riding somewhere about. He insisted on bringing his horse, Montaigne. I had to have a special stall built on the yacht's stern. Daucey's befriended some local baron's son. They ride together, and he often sails with us when we go out to sea. Even brings his own horse aboard."

Jessica choked on her tea.

"Are you all right, child?" the count inquired.

"Aunt Bet." Jessica gave Elizabeth a hard look.

"Oh dear, I—no, I cannot."

"Aunt Bet, you must."

"Whatever are you speaking about?" The count looked at them questioningly.

"Oh, dear," Elizabeth repeated, but at Jessica's frown went on. "I'm afraid we probably have disturbing news for you about your nephew, but then perhaps not. Surely it need not necessarily be him?" Elizabeth looked beseechingly at Jessica.

Jessica sighed. "Sir, there have been robberies along the coastal highway here for the past two weeks. Two young highwaymen who vanish with no trace. That is why Aunt Bet and I are here. We thought they might be using this cove. The sea would provide the only reasonable means of escape, as the authorities have considered everything else."

The count turned pale. "*Sacre bleu*! Excuse me, ladies. This is terrible, but I must admit it clarifies some matters. I have wondered that the boys have often ridden hard and arrived here right as we're setting sail. But surely they could not actually be robbing people. Why, this boy, Richard Carsdale, seemed so polite!"

"Richard Carsdale? I am familiar with no family of that name. He is certainly none of the barons' sons from this area," Elizabeth declared.

"Are you certain? Oh dear." The count rose in agitation. "I am afraid I have failed Gwendolyn! I had promised to keep the lad out of trouble, and here I have let him get into even worse. It would kill his sweet mother if the boy has to be imprisoned—or worse."

"They have not really hurt anyone," Jessica added hopefully, "and have only robbed the wealthy."

"Thank you, child. But that is hardly an excuse," the count said. "I do care for the boy like a son—I never had one of my own. I suppose we shall have to leave here immediately." He gave a definitely regretful look at Elizabeth. "But first I must see that whoever has been robbed is repaid."

"Jessica, you have all those clippings telling who was robbed. We can give you the names and help you return whatever was taken. Perhaps we can still straighten all this out."

They all turned at that moment as a horseman approached. "Hullo, Uncle," an extraordinarily handsome young man hailed good-naturedly as he swung down from his mount. He carelessly dropped the reins and ran lightly over the gangway. "Well, hello indeed!" He stopped on seeing his uncle's guests. "Don't tell me these two lovely ladies just walked up out of the marsh?" He gallantly included both women, but his eyes were clearly on Jessica.

The count frowned angrily at the youth. "Come here, Daucey! Though I don't know if you are worthy of being in the presence of these ladies."

The youth shifted uncomfortably, his cocky humor suddenly gone. "Uncle, perhaps I should go below first and—"

"Come here, I say!"

The boy approached reluctantly, avoiding looking at the two women. "Sir, whatever is wrong? I know I am late getting back this morning, but—"

"Daucey, these ladies have just told me that two young men have been robbing people along the coastal highway near here. Where is this friend of yours—Richard?"

"Uncle, surely you don't think—"

The older man cut him off. "Don't try to gull me, boy. Had I not been so involved in my writing, I should have taken more notice of your activities. It never occurred to me you would do anything of this order," he said angrily. "I have gone to a great deal of trouble to protect you and your friends from the consequences of your escapades in Paris."

"But Uncle"—Daucey glanced at the two women with embarrassment—"we've not hurt anyone or really stolen anything. It was but a lark. Why they've even made ballads up about us—the 'Gentleman Bandits.'"

"Quiet!" the count yelled in such a rage that all three of his audience jumped. "I cannot believe that one of my own blood would consider—"

"Had not we best be setting out home, Aunt?" Jessica asked nervously.

"In a moment, dear." Surprisingly, Elizabeth didn't take the hint. "Maurice, would you mind, please? Now Daucey, what do you mean you haven't taken anything?"

"Richard and I, we just stopped the coaches, ma'am. We'd posture a bit, give the ladies some compliments, that type thing. We knew we could never be found on shipboard, and then when we vanished in a few weeks, we'd be legends—like Uncle Maurice's pirate, Romand." He looked hopefully at Elizabeth, sensing her sympathy.

At Daucey's comment about Roland, Elizabeth and Maurice gave one another a guilty look.

"That's incredibly stupid!" Jessica unexpectedly burst out, much to the boy's chagrin. "Pirates are only interesting when you look back on them from years later. They were nothing but villains when they were really going around robbing and killing people."

"But we didn't—" Daucey began, not knowing what to make of the girl's attack.

"Yes, you did. The newspaper clipping plainly said that jewelry and purses were taken from people; only wealthy people, but that still doesn't make it right."

"I never did," Daucey insisted hotly. "I am not a thief.

Those papers must have been about someone else robbing along that same highway."

"What about this Richard?" Elizabeth asked. "Are you sure he wasn't taking things? I suppose you were always together?"

"Richard wouldn't do that."

"Were you together?" Elizabeth insisted, hearing his hesitation.

"Answer Lady Trenton, boy," his uncle demanded when the lad remained silent.

"Not always. Richard wanted to take turns being the—bandit. One of us would watch the driver while the other played up to the ladies in the coaches. But surely he would not have actually *robbed* them."

The count looked at him in disgust. "I cannot believe you to be so prodigiously stupid. Where does this Richard live? Lady Trenton has already informed me that the scoundrel is not any baron's son."

"Richard is actually a groom for an estate near here," Daucey allowed sullenly. "Lancaster is the man's name," he added, and Elizabeth rolled her eyes at Jessica. "But Uncle, I'm certain this is all just a hum. Richard is a fine chap—I don't want to bring him trouble."

"Bring *him* trouble?" Jessica stood up angrily before the young man. "Don't you know they *hang* highwaymen in England?"

Daucey turned exceedingly pale. "Hang?" he asked weakly.

"Yes, by the neck until dead," Jessica added a bit gruesomely, having been horrified by her own visions of this handsome young lad turned into a horrid gallows-fruit.

"Uncle Maurice! You would not let them— We must sail immediately."

"Yes, I suppose—" the count began, only to be cut off abruptly by Jessica.

"No, you are not! Apparently your family and uncle have helped you run away from whatever ninnyhammer thing you did in France, and you have learned nothing. My lord," she addressed the count, "you should make him face up to his mistakes and right them himself."

"Jessica!" Elizabeth began in horror at the girl interfering in these strangers' affairs, though she had done the same.

"No, my dear. The girl is correct," the count said. "We have done exactly that, protecting Daucey from his own foolishness. Instead of learning from his mistakes, he just keeps getting into more and more serious trouble. This time, Daucey, you will make retribution for your crimes and find your own way out!"

"Uncle Maurice, they may hang me!" The boy was close to tears.

Jessica took pity on him. "We shan't let them hang you," she said, without authority to do so, "at least not if you quit protecting this thieving friend of yours. My guardian is the magistrate of this area, and I'm sure if we simply explain the circumstances he will, as a reasonable man, help solve the whole matter," she decided airily.

Elizabeth looked to the heavens. "Oh dear, Jessica. I really don't think—I mean Gareth is, of course, a fair man, but really, perhaps we had best handle this ourselves," Elizabeth said quickly, not at all confident in how her nephew would react to this rather eccentric French count and his havey-cavey nephew. She also, needless to say, was not all that eager to explain how they managed to become entangled in the whole mess.

"You mean we should not tell Lord St. John?" For some reason Jessica found herself extremely reluctant to deceive his lordship in something of this magnitude. The minor things, such as keeping their destination secret, had seemed only innocent fun. However, Aunt Bet was her friend, and she disliked going against her. "I suppose that will be all right, if we can settle it quickly," she finally agreed. "If I'm correct, there were only three persons who actually had possessions taken from them. Aunt Bet, you know all the gentry in the region, do you not?"

"Yes, of course," confirmed Elizabeth. "Now Daucey, you understand that you must take your uncle to this Richard, and if possible retrieve whatever he has taken. Maurice, I'm certain if we return the stolen articles to their rightful owners and explain the boy's pranks, they'll not press charges, at least for Daucey's part."

"It is a worthy plan," the count agreed after a moment. "I think we will immediately go apprehend this scoundrel before he has more of a chance to dispose of the stolen items."

"Of course, Uncle." Daucey didn't appear entirely happy over the whole situation. "Are you coming with us?" he asked the ladies, hopeful of continued support.

"Don't be ridiculous, boy," the Count admonished him. "These ladies have incurred danger enough by just coming here. How shall we get these names from you to return the items, Lady Trenton?"

"It would not be wise for us to come here again. However, there is an inn, the Mare's Nest, on the coast road. I've often stopped there for luncheon with friends when we were riding. We shall meet you there, let me see, perhaps at noon tomorrow?"

Chapter Six

Luckily Jessica and Elizabeth arrived back at Cantonley in ample time to freshen up and get settled before the return of the earl.

The two of them were innocently, or so Gareth presumed, going over Jessica's clippings in the downstairs parlor when he found them. "Ah, back to the mystery of the handsome highwaymen?" He smiled at their poring so seriously over the papers. Coming closer he saw Jessica was making notes from the articles. "Don't tell me. I shall guess. You've decided to become a novelist and use this as your plot?" He grinned at her guilty start.

"Well, this does sound as though it should make an interesting story, does it not?" she said evasively, relieved at his providing such an excellent excuse.

Gareth chuckled. "Obviously, you ladies have managed to entertain yourselves suitably today. I do owe you an apology, Jessica, for my absence on your first day, but one of our neighbors, Lord Lancaster, has had some unfortunate goings-on he wished to consult me about."

"Thefts, no doubt?" Jessica muttered dryly before seeing Elizabeth's stern glance.

"Why, yes, as a matter of fact." Gareth looked at her in surprise. "But how would you—? Ah, your highwaymen again?"

Jessica didn't respond.

"Actually, there well may be a connection," the earl continued, considering. "Often even when diverse types of theft are occurring in a particular area, it is the same band of rogues."

"Exactly what has been stolen from Lord Lancaster?" Elizabeth cautiously inquired.

"Oh, mere rubbish—nothing of any great value. Small items, easily sold, such as pieces of livery from the stables, that manner of thing. It particularly annoys Lancaster, as he has taken every precaution and even had his employees on watch, but things continue to go astray."

"Perhaps it is one of the employees, then?" Jessica suggested innocently.

"That was precisely my conclusion," Gareth said with approval. "However, Lancaster strongly disagrees. He puts great pride in his discernment on hiring workers for his estate."

The subject was dropped as the butler came into the room to announce dinner.

After a long, formal dinner in the great hall, Elizabeth was surprised to have Gareth suggest a game of loo rather than retiring to the library with his brandy and journals as was his usual wont.

"I prefer whist," Gareth mentioned to Jessica as he was explaining the simpler game to her, "but it requires a foursome."

Jessica had never played any card games but caught on quickly, and they enjoyed the several hands before Gareth called it an early night. "I'm afraid I still have directions to prepare for my estate agent before morning," he explained before leaving the two of them.

Later in Elizabeth's suite, the two women reviewed the notes and clippings. "See, Lord Lancaster's cousin Lucille from Middlesex was one of the very first persons robbed," Jessica said.

"I would imagine this Richard planned to rob his own employer's relative, and having met Lucille, I can't help but see why he chose her," Elizabeth sniffed.

"She must be a harridan, but all he took was one gold watch."

"Does the clipping describe it?"

"Not actually, just noted it had great sentimental value to the owner and was emblazoned with the family crest. It was supposedly given to her by some late uncle."

"That crest would be the Lancaster arms. I should be able to recognize it without any difficulty; if we should locate it, that is. What else has been taken?"

"Well, let me see. Harvey Smithson, a tradesman in the shipping business, had his purse with some 20 pounds sterling taken."

"We know him also. He hails from Brighton, actually. Gareth employs his services as needed. He travels this road often."

"What does he do?" Jessica asked.

"Oh, it's not his work that brings him here. He's stepping out with a widow from one of the nearby villages. On occasion he delivers purchases that Gareth has ordered, as it is on his way. It will not be difficult for Maurice to return his funds to him—and I'm sure, if we say the count is our friend, Mister Smithson will readily forgive Daucey since he values Cantonley's business." Elizabeth nodded in satisfaction. "Now, what of the other? You did say there were three persons robbed."

"Yes, the third and most recent was a young lady traveling with her abigail. She was wearing a ruby ring and matching brooch, both of which were taken. I believe I have that one here, yes, here it is, Miss Clarissa Chancey."

"Oh, my heavens, Clarissa! I had heard of her being accosted. The Chancey estate is only a few miles north of here. Clarissa comes to all the local assemblies. I recall seeing that ruby set often. The poor dear, it's likely the only jewels she has—she must be simply distraught. Regardless, I'm sure I will recognize them as well—though finding something of that value shall require a great amount of good fortune."

"Perhaps our 'gentleman bandit' still has the ruby set? I cannot fathom his quickly finding someone to purchase something of that value without suspicion."

"Surely this Richard wouldn't have been foolish enough to try to sell something like those rubies in this locale. Still it might be worth the effort to ask around the village shops."

"That's a good idea. Perhaps we should go in tomorrow after we meet with the count?"

Elizabeth nodded. "I didn't mention to Gareth yet that we're having luncheon in the village tomorrow."

"What if he offers to escort us?" Jessica asked, thinking to herself that she wouldn't really wish to dissuade him if he did offer.

"That is a possibility. I have not been apprised of his plans, other than meeting his agent early on. I know," she said smugly, "I could tell him we're going by the parsonage and shall invite Leticia to accompany us."

"Leticia?"

"The parson's daughter. She has a horrid crush on Gareth, and he really can't abide her!"

"Oh." Jessica hesitated. "Is she pretty?"

"Yes, I suppose, in a Reubenesque fashion, but incredibly silly. Gareth, of course, would never entertain a liaison that far beneath him anyway," she added unthinkingly. "Even though the family is heir to a barony it is quite a *damnosa hereditas* due to Leticia's grandfather's gambling in White and Boodles." Elizabeth went on for some moments, caught up in telling the scandal, before noticing Jessica's obvious lack of enthusiasm. "My dear, I am rambling on so and you look absolutely worn out. You had best run along to bed. I'll send my Teresa to you. We really must get you your own lady's maid."

Jessica scarcely paid heed to Elizabeth's continued fussing. Actually, she was suddenly more melancholy than fatigued, but she wasn't quite sure why. Only later walking down the hall did it strike her, as she caught herself automatically looking to see if there were lights on in his lordship's room. It was what Elizabeth had said about the earl not having any interest in a female of a low order. She gave herself a mental shake. Whatever was she thinking? Of course an earl, particularly such a wealthy and powerful one as Lord St. John, would never consider a woman— "This is ridiculous," she chided herself aloud to stop her thoughts. After all, just because he'd befriended her—he was really much too old—and pompous— She frantically tried to revive her earlier feelings against the earl but somehow found them gone. Instead she found an odd sort of emptiness when he wasn't around, and she felt a yearning to see him, even just to know he was near.

"You are being quite a goose," she informed herself forcefully. "You're an orphan—an illegitimate orphan as well! The earl is only being charitable toward you." Refusing to let herself think on the matter further, she headed despondently up to her own bed.

The following morning found Jessica in better spirits as she had the day's adventures to look forward to. It turned out their threat of Leticia's company wasn't needed, since the earl had risen early to meet with his agent and then had departed to London on some business. He left word he would likely not return until the evening.

"Excellent." Elizabeth greeted the news with pleasure, not noticing Jessica's rather forlorn look. "We shall not have that problem to contend with at least."

Gareth however had remembered to instruct the stable-master, and he could not be dissuaded from assigning a groom to escort them.

"Very well," Elizabeth said, finally giving in. "But do send Jem. At least he's not so impatient as George."

As their horses were being readied she whispered to Jessica, "Jem has his Mary Anne, who works at the Mare's Nest. I know he hopes to wed her in the spring, so I'm sure he won't be biding much time with us."

As a matter of prudence, the two ladies kept their conversation trivial during the ride to the village, although Jem rode the requisite respectful two horse-lengths behind.

When they reached the inn, as expected the young man required little encouragement to be persuaded to seek out Mary Anne. The ladies were than free to meet the waiting count without a witness to relate that incident to the earl.

"Ah, my dear. There you are." Maurice had obviously been waiting anxiously, as he came forward the second they entered the common room. Elizabeth blushed as he bowed and kissed her hand before directing the two ladies into the private parlor he'd bespoken. Jessica was pleased that Aunt Bet had herself a beau in this rather dashing Frenchman, but was also concerned that they didn't really know much about him. She had read her share of novels about unscrupulous men taking advantage of the trusting naiveté of a lady.

Daucey stood up as the ladies entered the parlor and gave a polite bow. However, he definitely lacked the confidence of the previous day, his dressing down by Jessica not forgotten.

Jessica took pity on Daucey and sat down beside him. "Please don't stare as though you expect I might bite, Daucey. I really should apologize to you for yesterday. I, of course, had no right to lash out at you as I did. I must admit it truly horrified me to think of you in the hands of the law."

Considerably encouraged by the pretty speech as well as awed by the lovely young woman professing concern for his well-being, Daucey relaxed and the two of them were soon conversing quite amicably.

The count and Elizabeth all but ignored the younger couple as they engaged in their own conversation. It was well into the luncheon before either of the parties finally recalled the original purpose of their meeting.

"Oh, yes," Jessica said, and removed the bit of foolscap from her reticule at the count's belated inquiry. "As I had thought, there were only three persons actually robbed."

After she detailed the robberies, Daucey grimaced. "Yes, the stories would seem to be accurate. Those were the three episodes in which Richard was acting the 'highwayman.' I still cannot credit that bounder doing something like this to me."

The court gave Daucey a grim look. "Let's hear none of that now. It was you who placed yourself into such a situation. You had no business out there with that malefactor even pretending to be highwaymen. You will be inheriting not only estates but noble titles one day from both your parents and myself—should you escape the gallows. I do expect you to be mastering at least some notion of responsibility to carry on your family traditions!"

Daucey shifted uncomfortably. "I know, Uncle. I never expected to cause such as this."

"Did you find Richard?" Elizabeth asked to lessen the boy's embarrassment at his uncle's lecture.

"No. I rode over this morning, but Richard hadn't arrived. The village family with whom he was boarding claimed he left last evening still owing them blunt."

"Daucey, at least, paid that debt to the villager," his uncle noted approvingly.

"That was most generous of you, Daucey," Jessica allowed. "Though Richard's private debts should certainly not be laid at your door, I can imagine the family who had housed him were very appreciative to be paid."

"What do you suppose caused Richard to bolt?" Elizabeth inquired.

"It seems there is a Bow Street Runner in the locality asking questions. Richard quite likely decided to depart while he could," the count responded.

"Oh, dear. I wonder whether he took the jewels with him."

They agreed Jessica and Elizabeth should visit the local shops to determine whether any of the items had been pawned. Daucey wanted to go with the ladies, but the count insisted on his accompanying him to extend personal apologies to the tradesmen.

After the gentlemen left, Jessica turned to Elizabeth. "Aunt Bet, are you not developing a rather quick friendship with this count?"

Elizabeth smiled at Jessica's concern. "My dear, you must trust my judgment of character. In speaking with Maurice, I find I know a good many of his British relatives. I assure you, his lineage is impeccable. For that matter so is Daucey's," she teased. "You two seemed to be getting on tolerably well."

Jessica laughed. "Daucey is sweet, but a bit too dandified. Have you ever seen such as those puce riding britches he wore?" she remarked, changing the subject adroitly as she didn't wish to think further on the subject that had kept her tossing about a good portion of the previous night.

"But Jessica, in the *beau monde,* he would be a tulip of fashion," Elizabeth said.

"Perhaps," Jessica admitted. "I must say, I did see worse prancing about London. But I cannot imagine a real gentleman, such as Lord St. John, going about in such attire."

Imagining her dignified nephew in puce trousers and locks arranged "à la cherubin" amused Elizabeth so that she failed to notice Jessica's changed attitude toward the earl.

By walking the short distance into the village, the ladies avoided having Jem accompany them. "Jessica, we shall tell the shopkeepers we are looking for jewelry items for our Great Aunt Hortense's birthday. That should have them bring forth the gold watch or rubies, should they have them."

After having made their inquiries at all three village shops without success, Jessica drew Elizabeth's attention to a stablehand in the street. "Aunt Bet, look!" She pointed excitedly to a young man she remembered seeing in the inn's yard.

"What?" Elizabeth peered at the boy. She had become a bit shortsighted lately, though she would never admit it.

"His watch—see?" The boy was fiddling with a delicate looking pocket watch as though trying to set it. "That doesn't look like something a stablehand would have."

"Indeed not." Elizabeth finally focused on the timepiece. "Come along." Elizabeth approached the boy, who having noticed their interest, began to move nervously off.

"Hold up there, lad, if you please," Elizabeth stopped him. "I would like to see that watch."

"It ain't stole, m'um—I'd swear to it," he blurted out. "I done bought it. Honest, I did."

"Of course, son. I didn't mean to startle you so. It is just that Miss Jessica and I have been perusing the shops hoping to find something of that nature for a relative's birthday. I only thought you might be disposed to sell it," Elizabeth explained soothingly.

The boy hesitated, obviously tempted by the chance to make a profit, but reluctant for them to inspect the watch closely, since he had his own suspicions concerning that Richard and how he might have obtained a nabob's watch such as this.

"Well, if you don't wish to sell—" Elizabeth made as though to leave. The boy stopped her.

"Wait, m'um. I, uh, I probably would sell it for a price. I just bought it myself from a bugger, er, beggin' y'er pardon, m'um, that is, a fellow passing through. I'd, uh, planned to give to my own sweet mother, you see." He warmed to his tale, giving a sideways glance to determine what impression it was having. "Sick she is," he added for good measure. "Had to pay all my blunt for it, so I can't let it go cheap." In his enthusiasm for the sales pitch, he handed over the watch for them to inspect.

"This is certainly a fine piece." Elizabeth turned it over so Jessica could see the Lancaster seal plainly engraved on its gold cover.

The boy watched nervously. "That there decoration ain't nothing but the maker's design, nothin' you need worry about. It says it's a good watch," he assured them, not able to read the scrolled initials himself.

"Of course," Elizabeth agreed. "Let me see, this would probably be worth a crown."

The boy's eyes widened at his good fortune. "A crown! Oh, yeah, at least. Might be worth a crown, six?" he tried almost wistfully.

"Very well. You do drive a hard bargain." Elizabeth took the coins from her reticule, well aware the boy had probably gotten the watch from Richard for whatever shillings he'd had on him. "You buy something nourishing for your sick mother, now," she instructed the boy seriously.

"Yes, m'um. Thank ye, m'um." He bobbed, grinning, before taking off down the road with the fortune clutched tightly in his fist.

"What sick mother?" Jessica laughed. "Surely you didn't believe that Cheltenham drama?"

"No." Elizabeth smiled, tucking the watch away. "But he probably does have a family somewhere he helps support. Beside which, Maurice will repay me."

"Now that only leaves the rubies to settle out Daucey's debts," Jessica said with satisfaction.

It was late afternoon when they reached Cantonley. Both ladies were thoroughly worn out, and though neither spoke of it, the evening found them both rather pensive. Jessica's spirits had sunk on finding that the earl would not return until the morrow, and Elizabeth was fretting on how she could even manage some socially legitimate introduction for her Maurice.

The two women consulted briefly on their plans for the following day over an early dinner. Elizabeth had arranged that Daucey meet them, as though coincidentally, on their morning ride the next day to exchange information. "As I'm sure Jem will again accompany us, this way we can slip Daucey the watch and find out what else has transpired."

"I shall be so relieved when this is all solved." Jessica sighed, liking less and less her participation in a conspiracy which would doubtless leave the earl aghast.

After bidding good night to Elizabeth, Jessica went down to the lord's library again. She already had several books in her own room to read, but liked being in this room, which reflected his presence so strongly. Knowing he wouldn't catch her, Jessica went over and sat in the high-backed tapestry chair behind his big desk.

How strange to feel such a longing to see someone whom she had been terrified of a mere few days ago. Jessica sat back and let her thoughts roam.

She had felt close to people before, though she had never known the love of parents or siblings. There were the Brantons who had raised her. She'd become close to them, and the laird. And certainly the Rougette sisters. And now Aunt Bet. Jessica smiled, thinking how quickly that lady had come to seem like real family. But somehow when the earl was near her feelings were different. Jessica tried to attach words to those feelings but found them indescribable. It was strange how just knowing he was somewhere in the same house made her happier. Could that be what love was? Jessica frowned. What manner of tomfoolery! She couldn't be in love with his lordship! To him she was just a child, though she wasn't that much younger than his silly Meredith. She was really quite glad that he wasn't marrying that foolish girl. But he would eventually marry someone, and it would be someone with "lineage"! Unable to bear her thoughts longer, Jessica rose abruptly and headed up to her room.

The two ladies rode out early the next morning, closely supervised by Jem. As planned, Daucey appeared from the bordering property, presumably on Cantonley lands by accident, and rode over to introduce himself. The alert Jem came up close as Daucey approached the ladies, but relaxed when Lady Elizabeth stated they had briefly met the boy and his uncle at the inn the day before.

Once Jem moved his horse back to graze, Elizabeth inquired how Maurice had fared.

"Mister Smithson was very understanding, considering

the circumstances," Daucey told them. "He didn't even want Uncle Maurice to return the monies when he found out it was really Richard who had taken them, but Uncle insisted."

Jessica sighed in relief. "Mister Smithson agreed not to press charges?"

"Yes, against me. He said he would not promise the same for Richard should they ever catch him. But I doubt that they will."

"Why do you say that? Is there something you are not telling us?" Jessica inquired, suspicious at something in Daucey's tone.

"I did ride out yesterday and investigate some more on my own," Daucey confessed. "I am almost certain Richard has boarded a packet to the Americas. The *Yorkshire* was in dock at Portsmouth. Several people heard him inquiring about it, and word was about the wharf that it was taking crew. I also discovered that Richard had a lady friend in the next village. Apparently he promised to send for her once he was settled in the colonies." Daucey hesitated. "I know what Richard did was a crime, but I have to admit, I would not like to see him hang. We had become friends these past weeks."

Elizabeth chided Daucey for his attitude toward the thefts, but Jessica, particularly in her current romantic mood, was more inclined to forgive the young man. "Perhaps Richard was just trying to get money to marry his lady and take her away." She had mentally re-cast Daucey's bandit friend as an all but desperate lover.

"Really now, Jessica—" Elizabeth began, but the girl cut her off.

"That gives me a thought." Jessica turned back excitedly to Daucey. "Did you learn this woman's name?"

"Francine—Casey, I believe was the last name. She's from a village called Heathfield, but why?"

"Don't you see? Richard couldn't have sold the rubies, or he would have had plenty of money and wouldn't have sold the watch so cheaply."

"What watch?" Daucey asked, confused.

"The watch we—oh, I suppose we haven't told you that part yet." Elizabeth handed him the watch they had recovered, as Jessica explained. "We bought it back from a stableboy Richard sold it to. So now your uncle can return cousin Lucille's watch to the baron."

"This is a relief." The boy gave Jessica an admiring glance, tucking the watch safely away. "Now if we can only recover that lady's jewels."

"That is what I was trying to tell you," Jessica continued. "I would vouch that Miss Francine has them this very moment."

"Richard's lady friend?" Elizabeth frowned. "But why would she have them?"

"If Richard really loved her and had to leave in a hurry, I believe it likely he would leave the jewels with her so she could sell them later to buy her passage. He had no time to take them to a large city and sell them and then return to Portsmouth."

"That is true!" Daucey agreed excitedly. "That is exactly what I would have done," he added, not at all deterred by both of his partners' repressive glances. "I will deliver this watch to Uncle and then ride over to find Richard's Francine this very afternoon."

"Wait." Jessica stopped him as he turned his mount. "If she does have the jewels, you must pay her a fair price for them."

"Pay her? For stolen jewels? It is not like she bought them, as did that stableboy." Elizabeth looked askance at Jessica.

"I know." Jessica was now well caught up in the romance

of the story. "But it may be her only chance to join her love in the colonies. Surely you and your uncle can afford to help?" she beseeched Daucey.

Daucey was taken by the romantic aspects of the idea as well, not to mention the importance he felt at having Jessica plead with him so entreatingly. "That is true." He waved aside Elizabeth's protest. "Richard was my friend. I should be pleased to help them," he said nobly, reaching over to pat Jessica's hand reassuringly, although the gesture lacked the desired effect as his horse sidled restlessly. "Don't worry, Miss McDowell, I'll take care of Richard's lady friend."

"Oh, my heavens!" Their tender scene was interrupted by Elizabeth's exclamation. "The earl!"

All three turned as his lordship rode up scowling.

"I thought he wasn't to return until tonight," Jessica whispered, only to be shushed by Elizabeth.

"I can soothe Gareth, you two just agree with what I say."

Gareth relaxed somewhat on seeing Jem standing a little way off with his horse, but he was still annoyed at finding the two ladies with this strange lad. Especially because the boy had just let go of Jessica's hand.

"Good morning, Gareth," Elizabeth greeted him brightly. "What a pleasant surprise that you got back in time to join us. May I introduce young Daucey Constaigne, over from the coast with his uncle, the Count of Augustine. My nephew, Gareth St. John, the Earl of Cantonley."

Daucey nervously acknowledged the introduction, finding himself more than a little in awe of the large, obviously annoyed earl.

"It is the most amazing thing, Gareth," Elizabeth said before the earl could question the stranger. "Daucey's uncle is over here sailing the coast for inspiration on a history he's writing about Romand, the Norman. Our very own Romand! We ran into the two of them at the inn yesterday, when Jessica and I stopped for luncheon, and spoke briefly with them. The count is also related to Romand. I cannot but think you would enjoy meeting him!"

Gareth finally got a chance to speak. "You and your uncle have been sailing the coast, Lady Trenton said?"

"Yes, sir," Daucey agreed hesitantly. "We've actually anchored in a cove near here on occasion. We only yesterday discovered from Lady Trenton that it is on your property. My uncle had intended locating the landowner to ask permission to search this area for Norman ruins, so it was fortunate we happened upon these ladies."

"Hmm." Gareth glanced at Jessica, wondering at her unaccustomed silence through all of the explanation. "And just where is the count now?"

"I believe he was taking the sloop down the coast to some village for reprovisioning, sir. I am to meet him back at the cove later this morning."

"Gareth, do you suppose we might invite them over? The count mentioned he would so love to see the painting of Romand when I mentioned it."

The earl glared at his aunt, but the circumstances afforded no polite refusal. "I would be pleased to offer our hospitality, perhaps for luncheon tomorrow?" The earl wisely decided he had best learn more about these two. "Tell the count he must plan to spend several days as our guests at Cantonley. He may dock his yacht in my basin."

Gareth described how to reach the pier, which was just a short distance beyond the manor. "Friday, I will personally escort the count and yourself through the Norman ruins."

Elizabeth beamed at the unexpected gesture from her nephew as the youth stammered his thanks. "I am certain my uncle will be more than grateful for your kindness, my lord."

After settling on the time his guests would arrive the following afternoon, Gareth was obliged to invite Daucey to continue to ride with them. Sensing the invitation was not overly enthusiastic, Daucey declined, and set off to retrieve a certain set of rubies before meeting his uncle.

"You seem unnaturally quiet this morning, Jessica?" The earl drew his steed up beside her mare as they rode.

Jessica, struggling under a fierce assault of guilt at their deception of his lordship, found it impossible to meet his gaze. "I just have just a touch of the megrim, my lord," she said.

"Perhaps you would prefer to return home?" Though Gareth's voice was even, he had easily recognized the falsehood and his eyes hardened. He had noticed her watching that young scamp ride off, and had seen them holding hands.

"No, I'm sure the fresh air is all I need," Jessica assured him, finally able to evince a smile. "I had not realized there were any Norman ruins on your property, my lord. Might I ride with you when you show them to the count?" she asked quickly by way of changing the subject.

"Of course," Gareth answered shortly. "I had expected you and Aunt Bet to accompany us." So, the child was interested in the boy. Gareth frowned. He placed his annoyance on the fact that he knew nothing of the men. "Daucey is quite a handsome lad," he remarked after a moment. "You enjoyed your luncheon with them yesterday?"

"Oh, yes," Jessica responded innocently. "Daucey does have the most amusing stories of his episodes in France—" She stopped in dismay at Elizabeth's look. They had only admitted to speaking briefly to the gentlemen at the inn.

Gareth raised a brow inquiringly at his aunt.

"Oh, dear. I should apologize, Gareth. I was afraid you

would be angry at us for having lunch with strangers. Really I am certain that when you meet Maurice, that is, the Count of Augustine," she corrected, coloring highly, "that you will understand. He is after all a perfect gentleman."

"I think I am beginning to understand quite a lot," Gareth said dryly, "the least of which is that I should not let you two out of my sight. But we shall see about your beaux tonight. I am afraid though, Aunt, that I am not at all pleased with this incident."

"I know it was not really proper," Elizabeth pleaded, trying to get him back into a good humor. "I must admit when the count mentioned he was writing about Romand, I could not resist speaking further with him on his research."

"No doubt," Gareth agreed coldly. "I only hope you haven't found yourself a real pirate, this time."

Both ladies remained silent through the rest of the rather tense ride.

Jessica and Elizabeth both took special care with their toilet the following day. "You look lovely, Aunt Bet," Jessica complimented her teasingly. "You really are quite taken by your count, are you not? Are you certain it isn't just because he is related to your favorite pirate?"

Elizabeth laughed. "Doubtless that has a great deal to do with it! Don't you think there is a resemblance?" She had made Jessica view the old portrait more than once.

"Actually, I find the count much more handsome." Jessica grimaced. "I never could bear the thought of men with all that hair on their faces," she added, referring to the pirate's full red beard.

"And what of you, miss?" Elizabeth countered. "You have changed your mind no less than four times on which gown to wear. I don't suppose that has anything to do with the dashing young Daucey?"

Jessica smiled a little pensively. "Do you think this color

makes me look more mature?" she asked Elizabeth of the full, violet-patterned gown that she had finally settled on.

"Mature? You look quite lovely. But heavens, child, you and Daucey are so nearly of an age, why do you worry? And from the way he looks at you, you could come dressed in sacking cloth and he would be impressed," Elizabeth said lightly. "Come along now, let us go downstairs. It will be wiser if we are with Gareth when our guests arrive."

On descending the stairway, both ladies were startled to hear gay feminine voices from the hallway below. "Whoever could that be?" Elizabeth looked inquiringly at Jessica. "Surely the count and Daucey would not bring anyone else?"

They stopped in disbelief on seeing the gathered company. "Why Elizabeth, there you are," Lady Summerwood gushed expansively as though they were long-lost friends, coming over to grasp that startled lady's hands. "I was just telling your butler, Javits, how delighted we were with your kind offer."

"My—offer?" Elizabeth asked in dismay at finding the whole Summerwood clan, especially Meredith and her insipid cousin Catherine, present.

Lady Summerwood laughed girlishly. "Oh, dear. Surely you have not forgotten you invited us to come visit?" She kissed Elizabeth fondly on the cheek, knowing full well she could not deny it. "You poor dears, you must be terribly bored, rusticating like this in the country in the midst of the season! But you cannot believe how incredibly hot it is in town. I told dear Edward and the girls that we simply had to seek some relief! That is when I recalled your most kind invitation. We knew how pleased you would be if we surprised you!"

"Well, this is certainly a—surprise," Elizabeth acknowledged faintly as Lady Summerwood gaily acquainted Jessica with Catherine.

The noisy confusion of the hall came to a sudden hush as the earl strode from his library with an absolutely thunderous expression. "Whatever is all this commotion?"

Lord Summerwood, who had been standing aside, now stepped forward uncomfortably. Although he had personally wished to come and speak with Gareth he had not been pleased with the idea of a "surprise" visit at all. Even though his wife had informed him that Lady Trenton had invited them, it had not seemed the most appropriate of times to bring his family. Vivian, however, had convinced him that he should allow Meredith to speak personally to the earl. "St. John, I apologize for the confusion." He waved the servants waiting with the family baggage further to the side. "My wife said Lady Trenton invited us, but perhaps this is not good timing. We can, of course, retire to an inn . . ."

The earl took pity on the older man, well able to imagine how Lady Summerwood had pressured him into his. "I wouldn't think of it, Summerwood. You are naturally quite welcome in my home." He gestured to his butler. "Javits, please show the servants where to dispose of this luggage. We were just awaiting some other guests who were arriving for luncheon, so perhaps you will join us in the parlor?"

"If you will excuse Jessica and me, we will join you shortly." Elizabeth grabbed Jessica and pulled her to the side. "Please, dear, help me a moment. I suppose we shall have to totally reorganize the table now."

The earl nodded as they left, understanding the dilemma the unexpected guests caused.

Gareth smiled a bit cynically as Meredith and her cousin ran up and curtsied gaily before him. Meredith was just presenting the girl when her father came over.

"Will you excuse us, Catherine?" After the girl moved

off, Edward looked sternly at Meredith. "I believe you have something to say to Lord St. John?"

Meredith colored. "Yes, Father. I was just going to tell Gar—Lord St. John," she amended, seeing the cold look in the earl's eyes. Suddenly not so sure of herself she stammered, "Oh, sir, I cannot fault you with being angry at me. I do wish you had just set me straight about Jessica, though I, of course, had no right at all to speak to you about it, as Father has told me." She glanced imploringly at her father for help. "I do hope you will forgive me, however. I shall certainly apologize to Jessica, as I would not intentionally have done anything that would cause her—"

"Meredith." Gareth brought her confused babbling to a halt. "I am afraid I have no idea what you are speaking of. Exactly what are you apologizing for and what did I not 'set you straight' on?" he demanded.

The girl turned pale at the curtness of his tone. "Why Jessica's—well, lineage, of course, that is—"

Lord Summerwood broke in, realizing his daughter was making a worse mess of the situation. "St. John, I must explain we all believed that fanciful tale Lady Anne Westley started about Jessica's parentage. I certainly never condoned Meredith bringing the matter up with you, however. I had intended speaking to you in private about it, just to inform you of what was being said, though I am sure you were aware of the whole situation. That is one of our reasons for coming here, to apologize for the part Meredith and her friends might have had in spreading the falsehood. Now that it is all cleared up, Meredith wished to make amends to Jessica as well."

"Yes, I have spoken to Mother and we've planned a ball just for Jessica—"

"Summerwood, may I speak to you in private?" Gareth abruptly interrupted the girl and sent her to rejoin her mother. "Now, Summerwood, there are some—

documentation—problems with Jessica's inheritance I have been working on that I had no intention of discussing with anyone, certainly not your daughter. In fact, before I left London, I requested records from Dublin that have not yet arrived. I was, myself, not overly concerned about the problem as I assumed my acknowledging Jessica's relationship would have sufficed," he said cuttingly. "Obviously the gossipmongers of the *ton* were more concerned than I, however. I would appreciate your enlightening me as to what has brought on this sudden change of mind."

The viscount shifted uncomfortably. "I assumed you had heard from your solicitor. I am glad, at least, to be able to supply you with the news you were awaiting. As I'm sure you are aware, the records you sent for from Dublin provided documentation of the marriage of Jessica's mother to the laird McDowell's son, Robert. Your solicitor has already received and recorded the papers brought back by your emissary from Ireland."

Gareth gave him a hard look. "I must admit to finding it odd that you should have this information before I do."

"It happens I also retain Stoutamire as he is one of the better solicitors in all of London." At Gareth's look he hastened to explain. "Please do not think the man was indiscreet. Actually, I fear I accidentally overheard him instructing his clerk to file the papers. I'm certain he must have a message on its way to you at this very moment."

Gareth nodded curtly, hiding his pleasure at the report. His hunch in sending Conners to research the records from that hamlet in Ireland had paid off. Somehow after considering Jessica's description of the laird's son, it had not been plausible that such a gentle, intelligent youth would compromise a young girl he loved. It occurred to Gareth a more likely course was that the youth had indeed followed his heart, married the girl in secret, and then feared to tell his father and fiancée.

"I am pleased that the matter is now clarified to the

satisfaction of my peers," Gareth commented acerbically. "You will excuse me for a few minutes. I should like to inform Jessica, as this matter has caused her considerable pain."

The viscount headed for his own wife and daughter with the firm intention of chastising them for the discomfort they'd put him through.

Gareth found his aunt and Jessica frantically trying to reorganize the luncheon table for double the number of guests. "Gareth," said Elizabeth, looking up distractedly, "are the count and his nephew here yet? I hope you know I never really invited the Summerwoods."

"I know. It required little to discern Vivian Summerwood's scheme. Our other guests haven't arrived yet, but they should be here momentarily. Don't worry yourself about the meal. Tell Cook to serve whatever is prepared and they shall have to be content. As the count and Daucey are our invited guests, however, you should place their name cards in the places of honor. I wish to speak to Jessica for a moment, if you can get one of the housemaids to help you finish this."

"Of course," Elizabeth replied.

Jessica rather nervously followed the earl into his library. "My lord?"

The earl led her to a seat. "As annoying as their imposition is, it appears the Summerwoods have brought some good news from London on your behalf."

"Mine, sir? What have they to do with me?" Jessica asked in confusion.

"Well, I recently sent a messenger to Ireland to investigate your parentage. I did not tell you, since I was not sure what he would discover. But from your description of your father, I could not quite fathom his having conceived you without benefit of marriage."

"Sir, I don't understand. What—what are you saying?" Jessica leaned forward anxiously.

"I have not as yet seen the papers myself, as I missed seeing my solicitor when I was in town yesterday, but it appears Mister Stoutamire has already filed into London records the documentation of your parents' marriage."

"Marriage? They—you are saying my parents actually were wed?" Jessica exclaimed. "Then that means that I am not—"

"You are not illegitimate," the earl finished for her.

"But why? I mean how—" she stammered.

"As I said, I have not actually even seen the papers, but I imagine Robert McDowell married your mother in secret after they met in Ireland. He was doubtless afraid to tell his father, as he was still presumably engaged to Lady Anne. I am sure he intended telling them, but unfortunately put it off until too late. I would not be surprised if that was what Robert was trying to tell his father after the carriage accident, but the gentleman misunderstood."

Jessica's eyes glistened with unshed tears as she sat silently for a moment. "It is all so very sad, the way things happened. If only—"

"I know." Gareth took her hand consolingly. "If not for the carriage accident, I'm sure your life would have been quite different. This whole situation could have been avoided, in fact."

At Jessica's worried glance, he clarified his statement. "I am not referring to your being with us, Jessica, but of your being put through all that you have recently, as well as being raised without the security of knowing your parentage."

Jessica smiled hesitantly. "Thank you, sir." She looked down at his hand holding hers and felt her cheeks flush. "Now, I might even be considered—more—eligible for marriage?" She dared not meet his eyes.

Gareth frowned, releasing her hand. She must be quite serious about the count's nephew to be worrying about her eligibility. "I'm certain the count should find nothing in your lineage to make you unsuitable for young Daucey, if that is your concern." The statement somehow came out sounding much more curt then he had intended. "Which brings us to the fact that our guests should have arrived by now." Gareth rose and directed her out.

Jessica's heart sank as she followed him back to the parlor. The earl said the count would find her acceptable for his nephew. Obviously he still just wanted to get her married and off his hands. What a pea-goose she was to have thought that he could ever be interested in her himself!

When the earl and Jessica re-entered the parlor, Meredith came over immediately. "Jessica, I am so terribly sorry for my small part in this misunderstanding. I heard what happened at that horrid Charlotte Camden's musicale! She shall certainly never receive invitations into our circle again. Catherine and I were just discussing—"

Fortunately at that moment the butler announced the arrival of the count and his nephew. Jessica, given a reason to escape Meredith's sugary sweetness, quickly excused herself to go speak to Daucey.

Several of the party noted Jessica's immediate welcome of the young gallant. Both Meredith and her mother watched with some relief, glad that the girl had apparently settled her affections in a direction other than the earl. Gareth, however, watched with considerably less tolerance. Jessica had seemed to have too much intelligence to align herself with such a popinjay. The earl stifled his thoughts as he introduced the guests to one another.

"Why you sly creatures," Lady Summerwood said, having managed to corner Elizabeth after the introductions.

"It's no wonder you rushed off to the country! A French count—and so handsome! Jessica seems to have found herself a beau as well. Meredith and Catherine are all a twitter about this Daucey."

Though fully aware of what Lady Summerwood was doing, Elizabeth did not deny the contrived excuse for their leaving London, knowing that it would help Jessica on their return. Jessica had managed to whisper the news of her parentage to Elizabeth, so the reason for the Summerwoods' visit was now clear. Lady Summerwood had doubtless coerced her husband into bringing them to allow Meredith the chance to apologize to Jessica and inveigle her way back into the earl's good graces.

With that disquieting thought, Elizabeth scanned the room and was dismayed to see Meredith, as expected, at her coquettish best, tapping Gareth playfully with her fan as she giggled and blushed at some comment. Surely Gareth wouldn't change his mind on that one again?

"Luncheon is served, ma'am," the butler announced to Elizabeth.

"Oh, thank you, Javits. Come, dear." Elizabeth ushered Lady Summerwood out first as the gentlemen moved up to escort them.

Elizabeth was quite pleased to take the count's arm and glanced back to find Jessica looking not so happy at Daucey's side. She was, however, pleased to note Gareth appeared totally out of sorts at having Meredith and Catherine on either arm. Elizabeth smiled. She was likely worrying about Gareth unnecessarily, at least from the look on his face.

Elizabeth quickly moved to separate the earl from the two chattering young women after they entered the dining room. Gareth naturally headed the table and she had arranged the adults down the right side. The count next to the earl then herself and Lady Summerwood. On the earl's left she placed Jessica, then Daucey, Catherine and furtherest away, Meredith. The viscount was settled at the table's other end.

It was soon obvious that Lady Summerwood and Meredith were incensed over the seating arrangements. Meredith even went so far as to try to have Jessica switch places.

Elizabeth quickly went over before Jessica could be coerced into moving and escorted the older girl to her assigned seat as though she hadn't heard Meredith's request. "Here's your name placard, dear. We must become settled as I'm afraid Cook has held lunch for as long as possible."

The immediate flurry of servants serving wine and bringing the first course of vegetables, capon, veal, and fresh trout, quieted the group. When everyone was served, normal conversation began.

The earl engaged the count in a rather probing discussion. He had not yet had an opportunity to speak with the man and was determined to form some judgment before allowing the ladies of his household further involvement with him and Daucey.

Lady Summerwood cornered Elizabeth into inconsequential gabbling of the London gossip mill. Thwarted from her plan to be next to Gareth, Meredith determined her next best move was to make him jealous and began flirting outrageously with Daucey, thus joining the siege on the lad already begun by Catherine.

Daucey basked in the glow of their attention and scarcely looked at his previous choice, Jessica. In fact, no one seemed to notice how quiet she was, as she picked despondently at her meal.

The earl glanced at her in concern several times during his conversation with Maurice. He had noted the other two girls' flirtations with Daucey and decided that was the cause of Jessica's apparent low spirits.

The count had mentioned that Daucey's pranks were the

reason for the boy's temporary banishment from France, and Gareth was building a good basis to dislike Jessica's *tendre* for the lad. He wasn't, however, pleased by seeing the girl so downcast and sought to draw her into the conversation. "Jessica might perhaps enjoy helping you sort through the records we have on Romand." He smiled as she looked up in response to her name. "She is quite a scholar and has evidenced an interest in writing herself."

"Is that so?" The count was immediately interested. "I should appreciate the help, my dear. I have tried to get Daucey interested, but at his age he has little mind for academia."

"But Uncle," Daucey protested, "I have managed to be retained at Eton. It's just those musty old papers and—"

"La, sir!" Meredith broke in, ever so politely. "You must not tease Daucey, my lord. And you, sir," she chastened Gareth, "if you make poor Jessica out to be such a bluestocking, you shall frighten away all her suitors." She clapped her hands delightedly. "Which brings to mind—Mother and I have such a marvelous plan for you, Jessica. You shall come back to London with us and have a proper season. Why Catherine and I have invitations to simply all the main events of the *ton*, and as our guest you shall of course be included!" She gave Gareth a conspiratorial glance, as though going along with his previous request. "Of course, only if your guardian will allow it," she added confidently.

She and her mother had actually come up with the plan as a means of enticing the earl back to town and winning his favor by befriending the silly girl. "With this Jessica being constantly seen in comparison with you, my dear," Lady Summerwood had fondly told her lovely daughter, "Gareth's proper choice shall become quite obvious."

The earl ignored the look bordering on panic that Jessica threw him. Though not at all fooled by Meredith's sudden noble gesture, this invitation could provide a temporary way of removing the girl from the young dandy's influence. "That is kind of you, Meredith. Perhaps we shall discuss it later," he commented, and changed the subject to stop further discussion until he had thought the matter out.

To Jessica, the meal dragged on interminably, with even her friend Daucey forsaking her for the gayer company of the other two girls. It was not until they sojourned to the parlor for coffee that Daucey again sought her side since Meredith and Catherine immediately gravitated back to the earl. Gareth, in order to escape, began to suggest the gentlemen retire to his library for their port, but Lady Summerwood managed to forestall him.

"My lord," she said quickly, interrupting Gareth's invitation to the men. "I haven't heard anyone play that superb pianoforte in Cantonley's music room since your dear mother . . ." She paused dramatically as though in recollection of the late countess. "If you would not mind overly, I should love all of you to hear Meredith play on it. She is so very musical, and our instrument is not at all up to her talent."

The group was thus obliged to all insist on hearing Meredith play, and Gareth, thoroughly displeased at being outmaneuvered, rather stiffly escorted them to the music room.

The company gathered in real admiration of the truly beautiful instrument. "I've only seen one of these before," the count remarked. "It is from that German company, by Henry Steinweg, isn't it? Prince Frederick just recently acquired one. Wonderful sound. But you say it belonged to your mother? I didn't think Steinweg had built them for so very long."

"In fact, it was the last gift I gave my mother, actually just a few months before she died last fall," the earl said after a moment. "I brought it back when I went through the

Duchy of Brunswich, on a business matter. That is where Herr Steinweg has his shop. The company is called Steinway now—apparently they anglicized the name."

"Oh, my dear, I didn't mean to bring up sad thoughts of your mother! Perhaps Meredith shouldn't?" Not truly concerned of anyone's feelings, Lady Summerwood sought to bring the boring conversation on pianos to an end.

"Not at all," Gareth said politely, seating Meredith on the tapestried stool. "Mother would wish the instrument to be played."

Lady Summerwood smiled smugly at her husband as Meredith flawlessly executed a selection of pieces. He had always complained about her insisting Meredith have the very best music teacher, regardless of cost. The audience applauded enthusiastically after each of the girl's choices. Even Gareth relaxed in pleasure as he listened. He had never before heard Meredith play, having always successfully managed to avoid the musicales Lady Summerwood arranged.

After finishing the last piece, Meredith moved away from the piano and playfully drew Jessica over to take her place.

"It is your turn to play now, Jessica." She was confident that if the girl played at all, Jessica's efforts would naturally contrast poorly with her own talent.

"Oh, you play so wonderfully, Meredith, I am sure we would all prefer you to continue," Jessica protested, though she actually longed to try out the lovely tones of the piano. She and Elizabeth had been so busy since they arrived that she had not even discovered the music room.

Politeness again decreed that the company insist on hearing Jessica, and she gave in without too much encouragement. She sat at the piano, and after experimentally playing a couple of chords, she looked over at the earl. "I have heard of Steinway pianos, but I never would have expected this. Even the touch is different and the tone is so incredibly lovely." Her fingers moved naturally into one of her favorite Haydn sonatas. Then, to the confusion of her totally forgotten audience, she skipped through bits and pieces of several composers until she settled in delight upon Franz Liszt's transcription of Berlioz' deeply romantic *Symphonie Fantastique*.

With the opening movement of introspective reverie, Jessica carried her audience gently into the lyrical tale. The poetic slow movements seemed to hang in the heat of the day, bespeaking love and life. Then as they built, changing into the vividly dramatic fourth and fifth movements, the present seemed to vanish. The tension grew, until the wild death and demonic torment of the protagonist Lelio at the symphony's end left the room in stunned silence.

Jessica looked at the handkerchief the earl silently held out to her for a moment without comprehension, before realizing her cheeks were wet from the emotions she had experienced through the music.

She smiled at him in some embarrassment as she dried her tears. "It is just so beautiful—"

"Indeed," Gareth agreed softly, almost bemused by the emotional ravagement he had never expected to experience through music. He took her hand and gently led her away from the piano, almost fearful that she might begin to play again.

Gareth kept Jessica's hand, tucking it over his arm as the others rose and began filing out, all talking and laughing again as though suddenly awakened.

"That child certainly has a—dramatic style," Lady Summerwood commented loudly. "I really think, with the proper teacher to give her some discipline, she might develop into a good pianist. My Meredith, of course, studied under—"

Jessica looked up askance at the earl when he held her back as she started to follow the others out.

"I just wished to thank you, my dear. I don't think I have ever experienced such emotional qualities of music before your playing tonight."

Delighted by his compliment, Jessica instinctively moved closer and she turned to him, her eyes wide and soft. "I—my playing pleased you?"

"Yes, you please me." Gareth smiled down at her and suddenly found himself caught in the sweetness of the face so close to his. Scarcely aware of what he did, Gareth allowed his arms to slip about her.

It seemed so natural and right that Jessica wasn't frightened, though she felt herself tremble with an odd, sweet weakness that swept through her as he tightened his arms about her.

"Jessica—"

She watched him in still wonder, her lips parting naturally in a soft sigh as his head lowered toward hers.

"Gareth? Jessica?" Elizabeth called from down the hall when she finally noticed the two hadn't come out of the music room. Her voice stopped Gareth only moments from becoming lost in the lips raised so temptingly to his. He reluctantly released Jessica.

"Come, we must join the others." He looked away from the confusion in her eyes, his tone almost brusque from his frustration.

"Oh, there you are, dear." Elizabeth came up just as Jessica exited the room. "Why Jessica, you're terribly flushed. I do hope you haven't become upset at what that foolish Lady Summerwood said. Heaven knows what possesses her to be so utterly tactless at times. Your playing was truly magnificent! I don't know when I've become so totally lost in music. Maurice, also. He has actually heard Liszt himself play in Germany, and was amazed at your interpretation. He thinks . . ."

Jessica smiled and made appropriate murmurings as

Elizabeth was joined by the count, who added his own effusive compliments. She didn't really even hear what they said as she fought the devastating need that had enveloped her after the earl had released her so abruptly. Oh, why had Aunt Bet called out to them just then?

Chapter Seven

Gareth, unable to sleep, contemplated the embers of his fire long into the hours of dawn. He now realized that at some indefinable point in time he had ceased viewing Jessica as a rather annoying child. Now suddenly he found her a very desirable young woman. Amazingly enough, not only physically but intellectually pleasing as well. Not to mention talented. He envisioned her swaying over the keyboard in total absorption, enraptured by the emotions of the music.

His temples again throbbed as he recalled the feel and scent of her as he'd held her for those brief moments. The earl's eyes darkened at those thoughts, and he stood up abruptly and paced to the window. He realized now that his annoyance at young Daucey had nothing to do with the boy's character. The very thought of anyone else holding Jesse or daring to touch those lips turned his thoughts to violence. He wanted her with a fierce protective tenderness he had never felt for any woman.

The Earl of Cantonley stood at his window watching the early rays of dawn on the ocean and sardonically acknowledged that for the first time in his life he was in love.

The next morning found what had been intended to be an educational survey of the Norman ruins turned into a day of picnic and frolic.

Lady Summerwood had high-handedly taken charge and no less than three carriages were to accompany the riders. Two were loaded with food, drink, cutlery, and ground cloths, and the third was "in case the heat overtaxes the girls and they should have to ride out of the sun."

Gareth's optimism on rising was destroyed on viewing the entourage awaiting him as he came down the manor steps. He had come to like the erudite count and had been looking forward to the day of investigating their common Norman ancestry. The earl also had anticipated the outing as a chance to enjoy Jessica's company without the exasperating Summerwood females about, having assumed they would arise late.

Elizabeth was almost pleased at the earl's glowering look as he approached her. She had not been fooled in the least as to what she had interrupted in the music room, and was quite jubilant that Gareth had finally found himself in Cupid's bower! Nor could she have chosen better for him herself, she thought smugly. She had suspected from Jessica's actions the night before that the girl had given her heart, and rather unwisely Elizabeth had then feared, to her nephew. Elizabeth knew better than to underestimate another woman and feared Lady Summerwood and Meredith's careful onslaught of the earl could indeed be successful.

Meredith was, after all, incredibly lovely and finely versed in the art of coquetry. While Jessica was—Elizabeth smiled to herself—well, Jessica was simply Jessica. There was all the difference between them as between a hot-house rose and a handful of daisies.

But Elizabeth was now sure Gareth had decided he wanted Jessica. And she had never known her nephew not to get what he wanted.

"Aunt, exactly what is all of this?" Gareth asked as he stomped up, angrily gesturing toward the mingling carriages, horses, and servants.

Elizabeth merely shrugged unconcernedly, as Lady Summerwood swept up, the lavender ostrich feathers of her bonnet bobbing dangerously. "Ah, my lord, here you are." She smiled sweetly at Elizabeth. "Now you mustn't fuss at dear Elizabeth. I do confess this is all my doing." She laughed gaily, and in indicating the crowd, missed Gareth's almost murderous look.

"I couldn't believe you intended to take your dear guests on some boring trek to look at old ruins, so I planned a *real* outing! The girls are all so excited. Oh, here comes our Meredith now." She pointed just in time for the earl to view Meredith gracefully descending the manor steps; an absolute vision in a sky blue riding habit, lips parted, and golden curls blowing lightly in the sea breeze.

Elizabeth could well imagine how that scene had been orchestrated for Gareth's benefit and began to worry again, on seeing the earl's obvious enjoyment as he watched the girl approach.

"My lord," Meredith said, and curtsied enticingly before him, "I am so looking forward to learning about your Norman ancestry."

"It pleases me that you have an interest, my dear." Gareth suavely tucked the girl's hand over his arm.

Elizabeth noticed the smug glances mother and daughter cast one another, but having caught the almost diabolical glint in her nephew's eyes, she relaxed and followed along in eager anticipation as he led the two women to a shade tree. "I must confess to history being one of my favorite subjects, and one I will be delighted to share with you," he assured the unsuspecting young women. "Of course, to understand my family's more recent history, you must know the beginnings," Gareth continued, smiling innocently.

"Now William the First, 1066 through the late eighties sometime . . ." Elizabeth had to turn away to hide her giggles at the look bordering on horror in both women's eyes as the earl began his lecture. "You must pay attention to these dates now, Meredith," he chastened the girl, whose eyes were already becoming glassy, "as you shall have to refer back to them to understand the social implication of the British people at this time, combined with the economic conditions which led to the—"

Jessica just then ran down the stairs and over to the group. "I'm sorry I am late, sir." She smiled a little shyly at Gareth before glancing around. "Is everyone else ready?"

"That's all right," Elizabeth assured her. "The count and Daucey haven't yet arrived. Gareth was just beginning to tell us of early Norman history."

"Oh, really?" Jesse exclaimed enthusiastically. "Have I missed much, my lord?" she asked thoroughly puzzled when Gareth and Elizabeth both broke into laughter.

"I don't at all mind beginning again," Gareth finally managed.

"This is all so very fascinating," Lady Summerwood broke in quickly before Gareth could start again, "but I'm certain Lord d'Albrette and Daucey will want to hear all of it. Surely we should wait for them? Oh dear, what is that silly maid of mine doing over there?" She looked vaguely at the group of servants awaiting them. "Excuse me, I must go check—"

"I'll come with you, Mother," Meredith quickly added. "I want to be sure Sybil brought my other bonnet."

Jessica watched the two hurry off, disappointed that they had interrupted the earl's history. Then she noticed the waiting throng for the first time. "Whatever are all the carriages and servants for?" she asked in amazement.

"I'm afraid Lady Summerwood got wind of our morning ride to view the Norman ruins and has turned it into a mummer's parade," Gareth answered wryly.

"Oh. I suppose it is terribly ungracious, but I should have much preferred to have just us." Jessica sighed, echoing the earl's feelings, as the count and Daucey joined them. Only Daucey was enthusiastic about the changed plan.

"Actually it seems quite jolly," he allowed. "Rather dull just looking at ruins. There are Catherine and Meredith. Come on, Jessica, let's join them." The lad took Jessica's hand, only to have it firmly removed from his grasp by the earl.

"You may go, Daucey. I wish to speak with Jessica."

"Uh, yes, sir," Daucey said, somewhat startled by the earl's very cool tone.

Jessica hesitantly looked up at Gareth after Daucey left, having also noted the coolness. "Is something wrong, sir?"

"No." He reluctantly released her hand. "Actually I thought perhaps you might wish to remain with the count and me as I fill him in on the history, since you appeared interested. Of course, if you would prefer to go with the younger group—"

"Oh, no," Jessica said quickly. "As a matter of fact, sir, that reminds me. I had, well, hoped I might speak to you about that—" She hesitated, and Gareth raised a brow inquiringly.

"About what?"

"Well, being with the group reminded me. Last night Meredith and her mother spoke of wanting me to go back with them to London. I would really prefer not to have to go. Unless of course, you really want to—" She stopped just before voicing her fear that he still might just want to get rid of her.

"Want to?" he encouraged.

"Um—well, have me go to London," she ended somewhat lamely.

The earl surveyed her a moment in silence, wondering if it was really the Summerwoods' company she wished to avoid, or if she still wished to remain because of Daucey. "I prefer not to make you do something you are against," he said, "but perhaps we had best discuss it later."

Gareth turned to the count. "Now, Maurice, doubtless you are aware of the basic Norman history, so I'll begin where our personal family records pick up. I should also enjoy hearing of your knowledge of the period."

Jessica listened to their discussion in quiet fascination, scarcely noticing how the earl quite deftly kept her next to him as their horses were brought over and the party began to move out. Elizabeth, who was interested in anything concerning Romand, and especially the count, stayed close to them. Lord Summerwood also joined them, as he found the conversation preferable to his wife's scowling continence after finding she and the other girls had been somehow shifted to the rear of the entourage.

Lady Summerwood was not to be outdone for long. As soon as they dismounted at the ruins of a Norman coastal armament, she brought Meredith over and they quite blatantly flanked Gareth on either side.

Meredith, having once again seen her folly, now displayed an excited interest in everything the earl said, even managing to ask some fairly intelligent questions in order to keep his lordship's attention. When they rode out again, Lady Summerwood had carefully instructed the groom attending the horses to have Meredith's mount right next to the earl's so that as a matter of courtesy he had to hand her up onto the horse. With that arrangement, Meredith had no trouble supplanting Jessica's place riding beside Gareth.

The three supply carriages had all taken the main road to

a prearranged picnic site next to the ocean. It was nearly right on the noon hour when the riding party came up to them.

"What a beautiful site," Meredith enthused to Gareth, hoping to move the conversation to anything other than the boring history she was thoroughly sick of. "I so love the seashore! As it appears the servants have not as yet prepared the luncheon, my lord, would you allow me to go wading? There is such a lovely beach here," she pleaded, purposefully putting herself under his direction, as though truly his fiancée.

"I am sure it is your parents' place to give their permission," the earl said.

"But I know they shouldn't mind if you are there to see there is no danger. Here is Papa, now. Sir, if Lord St. John watches, might we girls please go wading?" she implored prettily, including Catherine and Jessica as though it was also their idea.

"Oh, may we?" Jessica came up just then and unwittingly helped Meredith's plan. She had been longing to get into the ocean since she had first seen it.

The viscount, who seldom bothered himself with any decisions on his daughter, turned the question to his wife.

"Well, I suppose it will be all right." Lady Summerwood pretended to agree reluctantly, while mentally congratulating her daughter on the ploy. She was quite sure Meredith was more interested in showing her delightful ankles to the earl than getting in the sticky salt water. "Girls, you must remember to be modest with your skirts now," she chided appropriately, as the three ran lightly down to the shore.

The other adults all wandered toward the folding chairs set up under nearby shade trees, leaving Gareth to watch over them. It helped his humor not at all when Daucey came over and eagerly offered to assist in the duty, obviously pleased with the prospect.

The earl and Daucey walked down to the sand to watch as the girls laughed and splashed happily in the shallows. Gareth was scarcely surprised when Meredith, several times, managed to let out little shrieks as though having stepped on something while "accidentally" lifting her skirts much higher than would have otherwise been acceptable.

Daucey tried very hard to keep the appreciative grin from his face. He glanced apprehensively at the man with him after forgetting himself and chuckling aloud as Meredith once again flashed her dimpled knees. Daucey was amazed to find the earl was not even looking at her. Probably at his age, he'd seen numerous such legs, Daucey thought enviously, before turning his attention back to the scene.

Gareth was actually watching Jessica's enjoyment of the beach, while envisioning pleasant times for the two of them alone in his private cove. While the other two girls had kept on their bonnets to preserve their porcelain complexions, Jessica had tossed hers carelessly upon the sand. Her hair was now wind tossed, her eyes and cheeks equally bright as she swooped to catch something from the water, letting her hems become soaked. "Oh, look—Catherine, Meredith. Isn't this shell lovely?"

Both girls came over, then with real shrieks this time ran up on the beach away from her. "Jessica, that has something in it!" Meredith cried.

Jessica started slightly on peering into the shell, and Gareth moved toward her in concern. But she laughed as he came over. "Look, sir, what a funny little creature lives in here!" She peeked back in at the crab as it drew back inside the shell. "It's all right, sillies," she called to the other two girls. "He is quite more afraid of us than we of him. Whatever is it, my lord?" she asked Gareth.

"A hermit crab." Gareth smiled down at her. "It's a type of crab that doesn't grow its own shell. They are called hermits because they utilize whatever empty shell they can find that fits them."

"That sounds convenient." Jessica grinned and started to put her fingers into the shell, but Gareth stopped her, laughing.

"I don't think you really want to do that. They are not dangerous, but they can pinch."

"Oh. Can you make him come out? I want to see what he looks like all over."

"I'm afraid that chap wouldn't appreciate it very much if I were to pull him out. Here, if we put it down and keep quiet for a moment, he will come out enough that you may see him." Gareth sat the crab a little way from them and shook his head in amusement as Jessica casually sat in the sand to watch more closely.

"Whatever are you doing?" Catherine and Meredith had finally ventured over, not liking being left out.

"Shh." Jessica hushed them. "It's about to come out."

"Eiii!" both girls cried as the crab began to emerge. "It's a spider! Keep it away!" They both ran up the beach to Daucey's willing protection.

"Oh, it isn't—" Jessica began, exasperated because they had startled the animal back into its shell. But then as legs began to unfurl from the shell again, she backed away a little herself and looked up at Gareth worriedly. "It isn't, is it?" She didn't particularly like spiders either.

Gareth laughed and knelt beside her. "No, though they do have a lot of legs as well. Now watch." He pointed as the hermit cautiously crept partway from the shell again and began edging away. "You see? He's not such a fearsome looking creature after all."

Jessica inspected the crab a bit dubiously. "Not really. But he does indeed have too many legs for my liking."

Gareth chuckled and unthinkingly combed her windblown hair back from her face with his fingers, enjoying the feel of its silky warmth.

Recalling the last time he'd rumpled her hair, Jessica smiled up at him guilelessly. "I like it when you touch my hair—it feels so oddly nice."

The earl instinctively slipped his fingers down to raise her face to his before he caught himself. Gareth rose, taking Jessica's hand to assist her. "Come along, brat. I would imagine our lunch is ready." He was obviously going to have to declare himself quickly, Gareth thought with a grin, before this provocative girl drove him to a real indiscretion!

"Whatever were Gareth and Jessica doing down there on the beach?" Meredith's mother drew her aside and demanded.

"Oh, nothing to worry about, I'm sure," Meredith said lightly. "Jessica was showing him some disgusting sea creature. After all, Mother, just look at her!"

Both women watched as Jessica and the earl walked up the path. Jessica indeed was thoroughly windblown and sandy, her hems soggy and dragging. Her cheeks were also quite unstylishly pink from the sun. Lady Summerwood relaxed on comparing the girl with her own, still elegantly groomed daughter.

"Jessica, my dear girl," she said, purposefully turning the group's attention to Jessica's state as they came up, "whatever have you been about? Why, you are all sandy. Your dress is simply soaked, and your hair! Put your bonnet back on immediately, child! You are going to have even more of those horrid freckles!"

Elizabeth stood up in fury at the hurt she saw come into Jessica's eyes as the girl self-consciously tried to confine her riotous hair under the sun bonnet, but Gareth stepped in.

"Madam," he said cuttingly to Lady Summerwood, "I am quite capable of directing my . . . ward," he finally finished. Turning to Jessica, he gently removed the bonnet from her hand and tossed it onto a chair. "My dear, you don't have to wear that if you don't wish to. I find your freckles charming—and I do quite enjoy your hair," he added meaningfully.

Jessica gave him such an ecstatic smile of love that the earl had to turn away for a moment to keep his own demeanor. He took her hand, and led her smiling to the prepared tables. "Come, let us be seated."

Meredith merely looked dumbstruck, but her mother's eyes turned to icy fury. That little nobody wasn't going to supplant her daughter! Lady Summerwood had confidently suggested to all her *amis intime* in London that they would be seeing Meredith's wedding date appearing in the papers when they returned. She was not going to let this chit make her a laughingstock. This Irish miss was going to find herself out of the running for Countess of Cantonley! However, she would have to move quickly, Lady Summerwood realized, because from the look in the earl's eyes, he was liable to be declaring himself very soon. In fact, her heart had almost stopped when he had hesitated before saying his "ward." She sensed that he had strongly considered another designation. Lady Summerwood's gaze turned speculatively to young Daucey, who had been flirting with Catherine and had noticed none of the previous scene.

Unfortunately, no one noticed the calculating gleam in Lady Summerwood's eye, as they enjoyed the lavish meal that was more feast than "picnic."

Elizabeth was almost alarmed at the ardor she saw in her nephew's eyes. He scarcely looked at anyone but Jessica during the meal. Maurice noticed and speculatively raised a brow at her.

"I know." Elizabeth chuckled quietly. "I think I had best start arranging a wedding rather quickly."

"That might be wise," he agreed wryly. "Is there a chance I could talk you into making it a double wedding?

Those two, after all, aren't going to be needing you much longer, and I happen to know of a gentleman who very much does."

"Maurice!" Elizabeth exclaimed in surprise. "Why sir, we have only known each other—"

"But I was sure of my feelings the first moment I saw you. My dear Elizabeth, I realize I am not handling this at all conventionally, but I have never much cared for convention. I believe you are similarly inclined. I hope I am not mistaken?" he asked in concern.

Elizabeth placed her hand in his out of sight under the table. "You are not at all mistaken, sir. I think I, too, have known since we first met." She hesitated. "But, there is the matter of Gareth. He was not quite comfortable with the idea of my French count."

Maurice reassured her. "I expect your nephew will have no objections. We have actually gotten on very well, and he has tentatively accepted an invitation to the Somme to view my own collection of our ancestral papers."

"Really?" Elizabeth was pleased. "But—well, Gareth is rather a stickler for convention, and I think we had better clear this matter with Daucey up as quickly as possible. Have you any further news?"

"I think we have that matter solved," Maurice confided. "I haven't had a chance to tell you, but Jessica's hunch was apparently right. I had my man, Ormand, go with Daucey to speak to the lady friend. We have the rubies back."

"Oh, that is a relief." Elizabeth sighed. "I do hope it didn't cost you too much."

"That is no problem. I hope to be able to return them to Lord Lancaster tomorrow morning. I sent a message that I would like to meet with him, and we can only hope that he will agree to let the matter drop. We haven't had much time together; perhaps you would honor me by accompanying me when I return the jewels? We could stop at that marvelous inn on the way back for luncheon."

Elizabeth beamed. "I would be delighted."

Lady Summerwood heard only the last exchange, but it was enough. Very good, she thought. With Elizabeth out of the way, she could surely manage to get Jessica and Daucey into some thoroughly compromising position. And with Jessica out of the way, Meredith would have no competition for the earl's attention. Lady Summerwood smiled to herself, and with ingratiating sweetness began talking to the girls about what fun they would all have in London.

The rest of the afternoon passed in a happy blur for Jessica. Her only disappointment was that at the last ruin's site as the earl and count climbed a rather precarious tower, Gareth had firmly forbidden her to follow. As Jessica watched the men clamor among the stones, she felt that wonderful warm feeling sweep over her again. The earl loved her, she knew it. He had come very close to kissing her only last night. And on the beach, he had wanted to hold her, she was sure of that from that odd way his eyes had seemed to go suddenly dark. She grinned. Oh, how she wished they could be alone so that he would hold her—and kiss her!

"And what might you be thinking, standing here all by yourself and blushing?" Daucey teased as he walked over to join her.

"What? Oh, Daucey, I thought you were with Meredith and Catherine," Jessica said in embarrassment.

"I was until Lady Summerwood insisted on their getting into the coach. There was something they needed to discuss, she said, and *I* wasn't invited," he told her, pretending he was gravely offended.

Jessica laughed. "Silly. I'm sure your feelings were hurt for all of two seconds, which you doubtless deserved. After all, you have totally ignored me since those two came into sight."

Daucey grinned sheepishly. "Well, I could scarcely expect to compete with the high Earl of Cantonley, now could I? Not to mention that his demeanor became pointedly discouraging every time I got near you!"

Jessica giggled. "He thought we had developed a *tendre* for one another."

Daucey sniffed disdainfully. "Well, I was *trying* to develop one for you, but you were constantly either admonishing me or making fun."

"Oh, pshaw! What is the longest so-called *tendre* you've ever had for a girl? Perhaps half an hour?"

"No." He pretended to consider the question. "Actually, I think that little flaxen-haired barmaid at the Cork and—oops! Here comes the earl now, and he's giving me that look again. I think I'll go flirt with your aunt."

"I think you'd best speak to your uncle before you do that," Jessica called out as he retreated.

"Speak to his uncle?" Gareth inquired lightly, somewhat disturbed by seeing them obviously enjoying one another's company again.

"Oh, it was nothing." Jessica blushed, not sure if Gareth knew about Elizabeth and the count. "Were you able to get all the way up into the tower?" she asked, changing the subject quickly and adding to the earl's suspicions.

"Magnificent structure," Maurice interrupted as he came up. "I have found plans of that exact design among my family's papers. Apparently, the Normans constructed the same fortifications wherever they went." He continued elaborating on the subject, drawing Gareth into the conversation as they returned to their mounts for the ride home.

It was late afternoon by the time the party arrived at Cantonley. The ladies were all thoroughly worn out and retired to their rooms to rest before dinner.

Elizabeth and Jessica closeted themselves in Elizabeth's sitting room briefly, so Elizabeth could tell Jessica the latest news on the jewels.

"Thank heavens." Jessica sighed in relief. "Surely Lord Lancaster will not press charges against Daucey, then?"

"I think not." Elizabeth looked curiously at Jessica. The girl seemed awfully concerned about that boy. She couldn't still be harboring feelings for the youth with Gareth in the offering? But Elizabeth decided she wouldn't mention anything about that relationship, until she definitely knew what was going on. "I have some other news to tell you, also," she added mischievously.

"Other?" Jessica looked at her, and seeing the excitement in her friend's eyes, guessed the cause. "Aunt Bet, he didn't! You mean—?"

"Yes, Maurice has proposed. Isn't it simply wonderful?"

Jessica threw her arms about the other woman joyously. "I am so happy for you. You two seem so—so right for each other somehow."

"Yes, we are," Elizabeth said positively. "It's so odd, I think we both knew the moment we met."

"Love at first sight. It must be nice to know instantly like that." She thought for a moment. "But—could you meet someone and maybe not even like them very much at all at first, before maybe deciding you . . . loved them, I guess?" she asked, feeling a little guilty about her negative first impression of Gareth. "That is, you don't have to know right away?"

"Well, no, of course not," Elizabeth agreed, suddenly even more concerned. At first Jessica had not liked Daucey at all. "I expect Maurice and I knew because we are much older and have more experience, so we are both aware of what we want in another person." She intended to feel Jessica out, but just then her maid came in to help her disrobe.

Jessica was trying to lead up to telling Aunt Bet about her feeling for the earl, but gave up on the maid's appearance. "I will leave you to rest now, Aunt Bet." She kissed the woman gently on the cheek. "And I am so very happy for you."

In her own room, Jessica threw off her riding habit and slipped on a light dressing gown. She was thoroughly tired, but too keyed up to relax. Why did being in love create so many strange emotions? And why were there so very many uncertainties? His lordship could be so attentive and act so loving one moment, and then the next he did something to make her unsure of his feelings. After he had come back from the tower with the count, he had no longer acted as friendly. He had seemed annoyed at finding her with Daucey. Surely he could not think she would prefer Daucey to him? Daucey was sweet, of course, but she couldn't imagine herself contemplating marrying such a scatterbrain.

A tap on her door interrupted her thoughts, and Jessica walked over to open it.

"Lady Trenton asked me to see if you needed anything, miss," Aunt Bet's maid told her.

"Thank you, Teresa, but I am fine," Jessica said, then stopped her. "Though I could use something to help me relax. I think I am just overtired—some milk, maybe? I would get it myself, but I am already undressed."

"Of course, miss." Teresa smiled. The young lady was always so polite—all the servants liked her. "I'll fetch you a small bit of Lady Elizabeth's headache powders, also. Perhaps they will help." She started to close the door, but the earl, who was just passing by, caught it and nodded for the maid to go on.

"Jessica, are you feeling ill?" He glanced into the room in concern, having heard the maid's comment about headache powders.

Jessica, finding herself unexpectedly confronted by the

very man who was causing all her turbulent feelings, became totally flustered. "Oh, no. I mean—not now." She smiled, and then caught herself. "That is . . ." She became lost as Gareth moved toward her. The look he saw in her eyes was enough to break the already frayed bonds of his sense of propriety.

"My lord?"

"Jessica, my love." He closed the door behind him and pulled her gently into his arms.

"Gareth," Jessica sighed, sliding her arms naturally about his neck as he masterfully silenced further words.

"Miss?" Teresa knocked lightly on the closed door. "Did you wish your milk warmed? Miss Jessica?"

The maid stepped back in surprise as the earl's voice, obviously very annoyed, answered from inside the room, "Yes, she wants her milk warmed!"

"Of course, sir." The maid hurried down the hall hoping his lordship wasn't fussing at the poor young miss about something. He had certainly sounded angry.

"You aren't leaving?" Jessica asked as Gareth reluctantly started to move away.

"I must, my love," he said, but couldn't resist holding her against him for another moment.

"Oh Gareth, I don't want you to go." Jessica looked up at him, not understanding the aching need that seemed to envelop her.

Gareth gently disentangled her arms from about him. "I don't want to either, but I should not even be in here with you like this, sweetheart." He lightly kissed her again before releasing her. "You must rest. We will speak later."

Meredith and Catherine convened in Lady Summerwood's room for a frantic discussion before they sought their own rooms. "Mother, I'm afraid Gareth really means to ask for that little—" Meredith began frantically.

"Did you see—?" Catherine broke in.

"Girls," Lady Summerwood said, quieting them. "I assure you I am not going to just sit by and let some bluestocking school miss walk off with the earl."

"But what can we do?" Meredith wailed.

"We are simply going to have to disqualify Miss Jessica as Lord St. John's bride," Lady Summerwood said positively. "Now, after we spoke in the carriage, I came up with a plan, but you two are going to have to help me."

Before the hour was out, one Summerwood groom had been sent with a message to a neighbor up the coast who had been a school friend of Lady Summerwood's, and another groom had been sent on a very special mission into the village. After this was done, Lady Summerwood thoroughly instructed the girls in their parts and then sent them off to their rooms.

Once they were gone, she cornered her husband. "Edward, I do so love this part of the country. Remember that seaside cottage down here you were so enthusiastic about?"

"The Sethmore house in Kent. But you said you would never live in some remote seashore area," Lord Summerwood said with annoyance.

"I know, and I am sorry. You were so excited about it. It was simply because I had never really gotten to be near the sea that much. I've now found that I love it. Do you suppose that property is still on the market?"

"Yes, as a matter of fact my solicitor just mentioned it to me again the other day," he allowed cautiously.

"Why, that is marvelous! Since we're this close, why don't you get Gareth to ride over with you to view it in the morning? Since he is familiar with waterfront estates, I'm sure he could advise you on anything it might be lacking."

"Well, I don't think that's necessary, and Gareth has other guests to attend to." He didn't wish to impose on the earl more than they had.

"I'm certain that he won't mind. Actually it appears

everyone of the party except the earl has plans tomorrow anyway, so he might welcome the invitation."

"How would you know what everyone is doing?" Lord Summerwood asked suspiciously, having been caught up in his wife's plots before.

"Elizabeth told me that she and Maurice are going on some errand to a neighboring estate and then to luncheon. They are quite the thing, you know! And Daucey is taking the girls all out for a sail—"

"Not alone? I don't know if you should allow that boy—"

"No, of course not. The count's steward, Ormand, and Meredith's maid will be sailing. They are just going along the coast for an hour or so in the morning. I had thought since the morning was free that I might take my abigail and ride over to see Margaret Bessinger—you know she lives just north of here—if you don't mind of course."

Lord Summerwood assured her that he didn't mind, having been afraid she had planned to go with him. "Well, perhaps I will speak with Gareth about riding over to Sethmore. He might enjoy it, as everyone else does appear to be occupied."

Gareth agreed to the morning plans, though he too was hesitant to let the girls sail with Daucey. On checking with Maurice though, the count assured him Ormand was an excellent sailor, as was Daucey, and would not allow them to come to any harm. Gareth was no longer concerned about Jessica's being with the young lad now that he was quite sure where her affections lay. He decided it was probably best to keep both himself and Jessica occupied. He would speak to her about marriage formally, after the Summerwoods departed later that afternoon. It would be an unnecessary affront to Meredith and her parents to formalize his engagement to Jessica while they were in his home.

All the plans appeared to proceed smoothly except for the fact that Lady Bessinger, along with her husband, appeared at Cantonley an hour before Lady Summerwood planned to leave for their house.

Lady Summerwood greeted her with feigned surprise. "Why Margaret, I was coming to your estate for luncheon."

"Oh dear." The woman appeared to be quite embarrassed. "I thought the message was that we were to come here. I was so very excited about seeing you again, I must have read it wrong."

As Gareth and Lord Summerwood had left much earlier, Elizabeth graciously interceded. "That is quite all right, Lady Bessinger. Lady Summerwood, why don't you and your guests just visit here and have lunch? I'm afraid we've all made other plans, but the girls and Daucey will be back for lunch anyway."

"Why, that is a marvelous idea. If you are certain we won't be imposing on the earl's hospitality?" Lady Summerwood asked so sincerely, Elizabeth never suspected that she had planned for the Bessingers to be there for a very good reason.

Unfortunately, all of Lady Summerwood's plans went smoothly.

Meredith had insisted on their taking the curricle the short distance to Gareth's landing where his and the count's yachts were harbored. "I'm afraid I'm just too exhausted from riding yesterday to even think of getting back on a horse," she had said, and Catherine had firmly agreed with her. Jessica and Daucey would have preferred to ride over, but gave in; Daucey drove the carriage to the dock.

Ormand was waiting for them with the yacht in readiness, and the party began to board eagerly.

Daucey, as expected, stood aside to help hand the girls across the gangplank to Ormand. Meredith hung back until Catherine and Jessica were already aboard. Then as the unsuspecting lad went to help Meredith over, she suddenly screamed and there was a huge splash.

Ormand and Daucey quickly lifted Meredith to safety from the shallow water, but she was no sooner aboard than she drew back and slapped Daucey. "You did that on purpose!" she furiously accused the amazed boy. "He pushed me," she said, turning to the astonished watchers. "And I wouldn't be a bit surprised if you two hadn't planned this just to humiliate me." She pointed at Jessica.

"Meredith, what on earth are you talking about?" Jessica stared at her in confusion.

"I did not push you in, Meredith. You just slipped. I hadn't even touched you," Daucey said, defending himself.

"You did too." Meredith began sobbing. "And I'll bet your girlfriend—" she glared at Jessica "—told you to. She's been jealous ever since we got here."

"What?" both accused parties began in astonishment, but Catherine joined in.

"That's true. Why don't you two just go sailing alone? I'm sure that's what you want anyway. Ormand, please take us back to Cantonley!"

"But miss, I—"

Meredith began sobbing more hysterically. "Oh, please, Ormand. I am not riding with those two! And I am getting a terrible chill." She shivered dramatically.

Daucey shook his head. "Maybe you'd best take them back, Ormand, and let Miss Summerwood dry herself. Jessica and I will wait here. You can come back and get us after taking them home. We'll straighten this out later," he assured Jessica.

Jessica and Daucey sat down on the dock's bench and discussed the bizarre happenings. Neither heard the two men who came from the bushes behind them.

Ormand was only mildly concerned when he returned to the basin and saw the sloop sailing off. Daucey had left a note pinned on the bench explaining that he was taking Miss Jessica on just a short sail since the other girls had spoiled their outing. Though Ormand knew the count wouldn't approve of the boy out there alone with that girl, he wasn't worried about any real danger, since Daucey was a good sailor. He sat down to wait.

After thirty minutes, the sloop's sail still hadn't reappeared from down the coast and Ormand began to worry, but he waited almost an hour before giving up and heading to Cantonley.

As neither his employer nor the earl had returned, the only person he could approach was Lady Summerwood. Ormand found her having coffee outside on the veranda with her guests and the two girls.

"Well, did you bring those two back?" Lady Summerwood asked him coldly as he came up. "I certainly wish a word with *Master* Daucey."

"I'm afraid Daucey took the young miss on a sail before I got back. He left this note saying they would only be a few minutes, but they haven't shown up and I'm getting very worried."

Lady Summerwood took the note, and in his agitation Ormand didn't think to get it back.

"We saw them sail past here a while ago," Catherine said. "They seemed perfectly all right then. The two of them were together at the helm."

"Yes, close together," Meredith sniffed. "I'm sure that's why that insufferable beast pushed me in; to get Catherine and me out of the way so they could be together!"

Ormand shifted nervously. "Well, ma'am, I would really feel better if I could go try to locate them. But I need someone's permission to take the earl's sloop out."

"You certainly don't expect me to give permission on something belonging to Lord St. John, do you?" Lady Summerwood glared at him. "Besides which, I am sure they will show up soon. Perhaps they just caught the wind wrong or something."

Lady Bessinger spoke up. "It is not at all proper for this young girl to be out there alone with that boy, is it?"

"I would definitely not allow Meredith or Catherine to do something like that," Lady Summerwood decreed, "but neither of those two asked my permission."

Ormand realized he wasn't going to get any help from these people and was getting more and more worried. "If you will excuse me, I think I'll ride out to see if I can find the count and Lady Trenton."

Lady Summerwood just shrugged and continued her conversation with her friend.

Ormand intercepted Maurice just as the two were leaving the Lancaster estate.

Elizabeth saw him riding up first and had Maurice draw up the horses. "Ormand, what in the world is the matter?"

Ormand quickly filled them in on the whole story. "Surely, Daucey wouldn't really push Meredith into the water?" Elizabeth asked the count, but he just shook his head.

"I shouldn't think so, but I never really know about that boy when he gets riled. There is nothing to this bit about Daucey and Jessica, is there? I was certain she was quite set on the earl."

"That's what I thought, but I can't honestly be sure about Jessica. She hasn't said anything to me, and neither has Gareth, though I assumed it was just because the Summerwoods were still here."

"Well, I expect we shall find them back when we get there," Maurice said comfortingly as they proceeded quickly back to Cantonley. "You mustn't overly worry, my dear; Daucey is an adequate helmsman. I sure there is a very plausible excuse for their lateness, though he certainly shouldn't have taken the girl out alone like this."

"I just can't imagine what Gareth is going to say. I do hope they get back before he returns." The count privately hoped so too, though he said nothing so as not to further upset Elizabeth.

It was well after noon by the time they arrived at the estate. They were met with the unwelcome news that the yacht had still not reappeared. Before he left, Ormand had taken it upon himself to have a stablehand sent to the dock with horses, just in case the two landed before he returned, but there was no sign of them.

"I'm afraid this is becoming quite serious," the count informed Elizabeth. "They have been gone for over four hours now, and barring an accident, it is totally improper to them to have been out there alone for this time."

"Oh, I know. Lady Summerwood and her friends have all spitefully pointed that out. It's most unfortunate they were here. But Maurice, I'm really worried that something has happened to them."

"Now, my dear, try not to worry. I do think, with your permission, Ormand and I should use the earl's sloop and go out in search of them."

Elizabeth was verging on hysteria two hours later when the count had still not returned. Lady Summerwood and her equally mean-spirited friend were no help at all. Elizabeth would have been tempted to ask Lady Bessinger to leave except that her husband, who was amazingly quite nice, had gone with Ormand and the count in case they needed help.

"Well, I certainly hope those two intend to marry after all this time," Lady Bessinger said smugly. "I should think it will be well advised."

"I thank heaven it's not my Meredith," Lady Summerwood enjoined. "Not, of course, that she would ever do anything of this nature. But I shudder to think of her being about with that French boy!" She had previously sent Meredith and Catherine to their rooms, so they wouldn't be "exposed" to this type of thing.

"Oh, do be quiet!" Elizabeth finally had all she could

take from them. "I will not entertain any more of this nonsense about those children being compromised. For all you know they could be out there fighting for their lives on the sea!"

Just then the earl strode up. "Whatever is going on here?"

"Oh, thank heavens you are back!" Elizabeth flung herself into her nephew's arms. "It's Jessica and Daucey, Gareth. They're out on the ocean somewhere in the count's sloop, and they have been gone since this morning!"

"What? You mean all the girls are out there with him?"

"No, just Jessica. The others didn't go."

"And why are those two out there alone?"

"Because that Daucey boy pushed my Meredith into the ocean," Lady Summerwood said indignantly, "and as they had taken a carriage to the landing, she quite understandably refused to even ride with that terrible boy and had the count's man bring them home. Jessica waited with Daucey, and when Ormand returned they had gone."

"We don't know that that is the whole truth." Elizabeth glared at Lady Summerwood. "But Meredith did somehow fall in the water and then wouldn't ride with Jessica or Daucey, because she thought Jessica had put the boy up to pushing her, according to Ormand. He brought the two girls back here, and when he returned for the others, they were gone. Daucey had left a note saying he had taken Jessica for a sail and would return in a few minutes. Ormand saw the sloop leaving as he came up and waited for them, but they—never came back."

"Meredith and Catherine saw them pass by here—standing quite close together, at the stern!" Lady Bessinger put in snidely.

"Who is this woman?" Gareth glared at her, and Elizabeth explained briefly about how the Bessingers had happened to be there.

Gareth gave Elizabeth a grim look at the thought of all the

witnesses to the escapade. "Where is Ormand? I wish to speak to him."

"He, Maurice, and Mrs. Bessinger's husband took your yacht—I gave them permission. I was sure you wouldn't mind. They are out looking for the other sloop now."

Lord Summerwood, who had come in with the earl, but had hung back silently until then, stepped up. "It looks like a sail out there now, Gareth." He pointed.

They all gathered at the stone wall of the patio, watching as a sloop came into sight from down the coast. They waited hopefully, but only one boat appeared.

"Is it—?" Elizabeth began.

"That's my yacht," Gareth said shortly. "Lady Summerwood, I wish to speak to your daughter and Catherine in the library while I wait for the sloop to dock."

"I will not have my Meredith upset—" Lady Summerwood began high-handedly, but the earl cut her off.

"Go and fetch them now!"

Both women left, as Lady Bessinger wasn't about to stay without her friend, and Gareth drew Elizabeth to the side. "Aunt Bet," he said soothingly. "We will find them. There are dozens of perfectly logical things that could detain a boat. They could be caught in the shallows, have a broken spar—any number of things. But I don't like the fact of their being out there alone. Have you spoken to Meredith at all?"

"No, Lady Summerwood had already sent the girls to their room when I returned, and I have been here watching—" She finally broke down and started sobbing. "Oh Gareth, do you really think they are all right?"

"They have to be," her nephew said bleakly, unable to even think about the possibility of anything having happened to Jessica.

His short interview with Meredith and Catherine told him nothing. Both girls, truly frightened at his wrath should he discover their real part in the charade, merely cried and answered almost incoherently.

"I'm going to meet Maurice at the docks and go back out with him," Gareth informed Elizabeth, after he dismissed the girls in disgust. "I know the coastline along here better. I'm sure we'll find them." He started to go, but Elizabeth stopped him.

"Gareth, you—love Jessica, don't you?" She looked at him, worried about what it would do to him if they found Jessica had willingly stayed out so long with Daucey.

Gareth understood what she was asking. "Yes. And Jessica loves me. She would never have purposely stayed away with that boy."

Javits came in quickly as Gareth turned from Elizabeth. "Your Lordship, the count has tacked in close to shore—he called out that he has the young miss and lad aboard."

"Oh, thank God!" Elizabeth cried.

"Have the carriage sent to the docks immediately, Javits. My horse is still outside?"

"Yes, sir."

"I'm going with you," Elizabeth said, and Gareth didn't argue. "Lord Summerwood's horse will still be here, too."

Both Gareth and Elizabeth scanned the deck hopefully as his yacht slid into its bay, but they only saw a very grim-faced Maurice at the helm with Lord Bessinger beside him. Ormand was busy securing the sail and lanyards. He carefully avoided their eyes.

Gareth went over and caught the landing rope, deftly tying it off before the groom was able to assist. "Where are they? Are they all right?" he demanded.

"They will be fine." Maurice looked at the servants milling around the dock and gestured Gareth to come aboard.

"Wait here," Gareth told Elizabeth firmly, "and keep the

servants back. Where are they?" he demanded of the count.

"They're below in the cabin." The count hesitated.

"And?"

"They appear to be quite—inebriated."

"What?" Gareth moved toward the stairway.

The count followed him quickly. "Wait. We found the yacht anchored in the cove we've been staying in. I left it there as neither Lord Bessinger nor I sail—"

"I am not interested in your yacht!" Gareth cut him off as he flung open the door of the cabin. Daucey was laying sprawled on the sofa. "Where is Jessica?"

The count just pointed resignedly to another door that led to the bedroom.

Gareth entered the room and walked quickly to where the girl lay under a blanket. "Jessica?" He frowned at the strong smell of alcohol that came from the bed, then reached over and flipped the blanket back. The girl's clothes were totally awry. Her bodice lay open with the buttons mostly torn off, her skirts crumpled, and her stockings and shoes were missing. He stood frozen in shock for a moment before turning with deadly fury.

"Gareth!" The count blocked the door. "My nephew would not have raped her!"

The earl started to shove the other man aside, but just then Jessica moaned. Gareth turned back to the bed and stood silently watching as she struggled toward consciousness.

Jessica opened her eyes, but couldn't seem to focus on anything. It was all a fuzzy blur, and her head ached so abominably. "Daucey? Daucey, what happened?" She barely made out the man standing beside her.

"Daucey is passed out drunk in the other room," a cold voice advised her.

Jessica tried to sit up, but shuddered and lay back, closing her eyes as she drifted back into unconsciousness.

"Where were they when you found them?"

The count knew Gareth wasn't asking the sloop's location. "They were both in the cabin, passed out on the bed, much as Jessica is now."

Gareth nodded coldly. "You had alcohol aboard?"

"I stock wines. There were five or six empty bottles about the cabin."

Gareth stared down at Jessica a moment, feeling physically ill. He finally reached down and shook her. "Jessica, wake up."

"What is wrong? I feel so sick—" Jessica tried to make some sense through the heavy fog that still settled over her mind.

"You have apparently gotten quite drunk, along with your beau!"

"What?" She finally forced herself to focus on him. "Gareth? Sir? Why are you here? And what do you mean drunk—what are you talking about? Please, my head it feels so—heavy . . ." She tried to lie back, but he wouldn't let her. "Where am I? This isn't Cantonley?"

"You're on my yacht. The count left his where Daucey anchored it."

"Anchored it?" Jessica practically forced her mind to clear. "We weren't on the count's yacht, we were—waiting for the carriage to come back!"

The count gave Gareth a sharp look and came over. "We found you and Daucey on my yacht, anchored in the cove."

"We didn't go sailing—Meredith—they wouldn't—" Jessica tried to speak through the pain in her head.

"What happened to you then?" Gareth steadied her as she swayed again and raised her face to make her look at him.

"Please, sir." Jessica tried to brush his hand away. "My face, it—it hurts."

Gareth tilted her face to the light and cursed. "What are these bruises?"

"Bruises? Something—something was over my mouth," she said, remembering. "It was pressed so hard and had this horrid smell."

The two men looked at each other. "Go check Daucey," Gareth commanded as he wrapped Jessica in the blanket and lifted her.

The count had Daucey standing up weakly as he tried to find out what had happened. When Gareth carried Jessica from the bedroom, the boy cried out, "Jessica? Is she all right?" He tried to move toward her, but the count stopped him.

"Did he tell you anything?" Gareth asked.

"The same thing. Apparently they were drugged and rendered unconscious. He didn't know they were even on the boat."

Elizabeth rushed over as Gareth came up carrying Jessica. "Oh, dear God, she's not—"

"She's—ill. Send for the doctor immediately," he said grimly as he placed her carefully on the coach seat. The count guided Daucey over, the boy leaning weakly on him. The earl nodded for Maurice to place him in the carriage also. "I have sent for a doctor for them. After we leave, search this area for any signs of struggle or drugs. Were there any valuables taken from your yacht?" he quietly asked the count.

"I didn't even check. We just carried the children aboard and headed back."

"Perhaps you could send Ormand. My groom Henry is a good seaman and trustworthy. He can go with him to return your craft."

They arrived back at Cantonley to find that Lady Bessinger had ordered her coach brought around and was only waiting for her husband in order to depart. She and all the

Summerwoods were standing on the manor steps when Gareth carried Jessica up, with Daucey struggling behind on the coachman's arm.

Lady Bessinger sniffed as they passed. "Drunk! I can't believe it. Harvey, I think I've seen enough. I believe we should go," she told her husband stiffly as he came up.

Gareth didn't even turn. "Javits, have the grooms see that no one leaves this property. I would like to have all my guests convene in my library in half an hour."

The earl lay Jessica gently on her bed and deftly removed the torn, wine-soaked dress himself, as he hadn't allowed thc maid in. He tossed it down with the blanket to dispose of later.

"Gareth?" Elizabeth knocked on the door.

He pulled back the covers and tucked Jessica under them. Then he opened the door for his aunt.

"They—they were drunk?" Elizabeth whispered in horror as the girl dozed.

"No, they were kidnapped and drugged. The only alcohol was that poured on their clothes to make it appear as though they were drunk."

Elizabeth gasped and then noticed the torn dress on the floor. "Oh, no, Gareth! She wasn't—"

"I don't know," he said bleakly. "Stay with her, Aunt, until the doctor arrives." He wrapped the dress in the blanket and strode out.

After checking to see that Daucey was being looked after by Javits, Gareth went into his own room. He temporarily disposed of the rather damning evidence of the dress in the corner of an armoire and then, leaning upon it, closed his eyes for a moment.

There was no trace of the near devastation he felt on his face as he left the room and went back down to where his guests were angrily convened.

"I will not be held prisoner at any man's home. Even if

he is an earl," Gareth heard Lady Bessinger say as he hesitated at the library door.

A sudden hush fell as the earl entered. "No one is being held prisoner," he said evenly. "I merely wish to speak to you before you depart."

Lady Bessinger sniffed, but kept silent when her husband frowned heavily at her.

"I was sure you would all be anxious to know that my ward and Daucey Constaigne are going to be fine. It appears they were accosted by footpads as they waited for the carriage to come pick them up." He gave Meredith and Catherine a cold look. "The thieves forced them to take the yacht out, and after looting it, anchored it in a cove down the coast. It seems they tied Jessica and Daucey up in the cabin." He then gave Lord Bessinger a hard look, hoping he would be gentleman enough to go along with the story. He knew Maurice had asked the man to say nothing.

"Fortunately, neither of the pair are seriously injured, though both are quite understandably overcome by the trauma."

"Surely you don't really expect this mysterious footpad story to be taken seriously!" Lady Summerwood snapped. "Just marry the couple off without trying to insult our intelligence. It's plain as a pikestaff what really happened here. Those two absolutely reek of alcohol."

The earl gave Lady Summerwood an icy stare. "You are perhaps more enlightened on the situation than I, madam?"

Lady Summerwood suddenly paled.

"I must apologize for my wife," Lord Summerwood quickly replied, glaring at her. "I am sure we are all quite glad the two young people have returned safely."

Chapter Eight

After the others filed out, Gareth drew Lord Bessinger to one side. "I hope you can understand my reasons for telling the group what I did. Jessica has been through enough without having any worse speculations loosed to the gossip mongers of London."

"Of course," the man agreed readily. "It is a terrible situation. She is such a young girl." The man shook his head. "But you may trust I will go along with whatever you deem prudent."

"Thank you," Gareth said simply. "I am equally certain I can rely on the count and his man, Ormand; so perhaps I can shield Jessica from the worst." He sighed, knowing there was no real way he could keep the women from intimating all manner of things among the *ton*.

Lady Summerwood looked up with absolute venom as the two men came from the earl's library. So he had coerced that spineless husband of Margaret's into agreeing to his story! Well, he should have left well enough alone and simply married the girl off to Daucey. She had told the two ruffians she'd hired to make sure the girl's clothes were sufficiently disarrayed to seal the girl's fate. Now with the earl's story of footpads and Jessica being tied up, it would appear as though the thieves raped her—and, suspecting that, Daucey's family would not even let him marry her. Too bad, but it was Gareth's own doing. Lady Summerwood turned sweetly to the earl.

"Oh, my lord, it is such a pity that you went and told everyone that those children were tied up."

Before he could reply, Javits appeared. "Your Lordship, excuse me. There are two Bow Street men here to see you—they've caught those highwaymen."

Gareth frowned. "Not just now, Javits. Have them deliver the men to the sheriff. I will ride in later." He waved the man away.

Lord Summerwood, who knew nothing but Gareth's version of the sailing incident, stepped up. "Wait, Javits. St. John, please excuse me, but don't you suppose there's a chance these might be the same two that waylaid the children? It is in the same area."

"Thank you, Summerwood." Gareth ran his hand distractedly through his hair. "I'm afraid I am not thinking logically. Yes, have them brought to the library." He almost dreaded the confirmation. If they were the ones who took Jessica and Daucey and had molested Jessica, he would kill them!

Lady Summerwood, realizing Gareth had forgotten what she'd said before Javits came in, remarked loudly to Lady Bessinger, "This is so terribly tragic for that poor girl. With her garments—all torn open like that—and by footpads. Oh, how I wish it had only been a liaison between the two youths!"

Gareth turned in fury as everyone looked aghast at her

statement. "You had no way of seeing her garments—I had wrapped her in a blanket to ward off shock."

She backed away at his anger but wouldn't give up. "My lord! There were a dozen servants at the docks, and you know how they talk. Of course it's very noble of you, but—"

"Vivian!" Lord Summerwood came over quickly and furiously pulled his wife off to the side.

Gareth took a deep breath to try and compose himself. That utter witch! Half a dozen people had heard her, the worst being Meredith, Catherine and that bloody Lady Bessinger. But how in the hell had she known about Jessica's clothes being torn, as he had indeed wrapped her in the blanket before removing her from the sloop?

"My lord, here are the Runners with their prisoners," Javits informed him hesitantly.

"Y'er Lordship!" Angus Conners came up smiling, innocently unaware of all that was going on. "I think we've got your highwaymen for you, sir."

"We ain't no 'ighwaymen!" One of the rough looking men stepped forward anxiously. "We ain't, sir. We was, uh, just crossing the property—we ain't robbed nobody."

Gareth was surprised to see Lady Summerwood whirl about and look at the man before turning quickly away. The earl stared at her. She wouldn't have—?

"Should I take them on to y'er libr'y, sir?" Conners asked.

"No, I'll speak to them here," Gareth said coldly. If Lady Summerwood had in fact done what he was beginning to suspect she had, he was going to find out here and now.

"Are you men aware that robbing people on the highways is a felonious offense against the Crown, punishable by hanging?" he asked sternly. "And, I might add, as magistrate of this area I am not known to be lenient in such cases."

"Oh, God, sir. Y'er Lordship—sir! We ain't robbed nobody! We ain't no 'ighwaymen, no, ye gotta believe us!"

"Then just what were you doing on my estate?"

"Nothing, sir, Y'er Lordship. We was just passin'—I know we shouldn't of been on y'er property, but—we was just passin'," the older of the two said quickly, thinking for sure they had gotten away with the other thing. They had kept those two unconscious the whole time so they couldn't have seen anything. They would have gotten away clean except for those bloody Bow Streeters lurking about.

"Your lying shall be the death of you," Gareth informed them coldly. "You are not only highwaymen, but I have it on very good authority that you have also kidnapped two young people and robbed my good friend's yacht. Yes, indeed, you both shall surely hang."

Lady Summerwood stared at Gareth.

"No! No, we ain't them! We ain't robbed nothin', nor hurt nobody!"

"I also know you have an accomplice in this very room—" Gareth ignored the gasps from the watchers "—and the only way you may have any chance of saving your sorry hides is for me to find out the truth. Do you understand what I've said?"

"No, sir—I mean, yes, sir, Y'er Lordship. We didn't have—" the older man began, but the other broke in.

"Cal, I ain't gonna swing—I done watched as my own cousin jerked on the rope—I ain't gonna swing for no woman!"

"Shut up, Nevin, you fool!" The other man poked at him.

"I ain't—that woman there, Y'er Lordship—" he declared, pointing out Lady Summerwood. "She paid us, she did. Paid us to do it!"

All eyes turned in horror to Lady Summerwood, who fell to the floor in a very real faint.

Gareth ignored her. "Very well, I do believe you aren't the highwaymen then, but the young woman on board that yacht happened to be my ward—and my fiancée!" he added, and the listeners again gasped.

"Oh merciful Chri—" The older man stopped himself seeing his death plainly in Gareth's eyes. "We ain't hurt the gel! Honest to God, we ain't hurt her none! That woman, she said to make it look like they had done—like that pair had done been together." He was visibly shaking. "She said them two was wanting to marry anyway, but the gel's guardian wouldn't let her, and if they was to be found together like, he'd have to marry 'em right off! Please, Y'er Lordship, surely you ain't goin' to hang us for such?"

Gareth steadied himself. "My fiancée's apparel was torn and in disarray," he stated coldly.

"Oh, dear God!" The man fell to his knees fully knowing what a charge of rape meant. "We ain't! Honest to Aw-'mighty God, we never touched that gel, Y'er Lordship. We wouldn't rape no young gel! Honest to God, sir! That woman"—he pointed frantically to the prostrate Lady Summerwood—"she said we was to muss up the gel's clothes and pour wine about them, but we ain't touched that gel. I swear to ye on me mother's grave, sir! We just put them out with some ether—hell, that don't hurt them none. I only pulled off a few buttons—and—and crumpled her clothes a little," he added. "Honest, sir—I ain't so much as looked at her, sir. Why, I looked away, I did—"

The younger man whined frantically in agreement.

Gareth felt the great weight of concern release his heart. He was quite sure these two really wouldn't have molested a gentlewoman. He directed the two Bow Street men to take the prisoners, still babbling, outside.

Lord Summerwood was absolutely ashen as the earl turned back to them. He ignored Lady Summerwood who had revived but was sobbing hysterically. Lady Bessinger tugged frantically on her husband's sleeve. "Let's leave, Harvey—we've got to leave now."

"I think not, Lady Bessinger." Gareth looked at her in disgust. "It appears to me awfully coincidental that you just happened to mix up directions and be here, uninvited, at my house as witness to this charade."

Lord Bessinger looked at his wife angrily. "Margaret! Did you know what Lady Summerwood invited us over here for?" Seeing the truth in the fear in the woman's eyes, he turned to Gareth grimly. "I knew nothing of this, sir. I would never have allowed my wife—"

"I know." Gareth cut him off. "I also know you are not involved in this, Summerwood. However, I would like to speak to you both in my library."

Immediately after the earl's conference with the two men, the Summerwoods and the Bessingers quickly departed.

The earl then proceeded back upstairs where the physician was with Jessica and Daucey. Though he had been reasonably sure they were both doing well, it was still a relief when it was confirmed. Gareth was particularly concerned about Jessica.

"She should sleep most of the day, and I would keep her in bed at least until tomorrow as she might be a little dizzy and nauseated from being kept out by the ether for all those hours, but I don't foresee that she will suffer any lasting aftereffects. As for the—other—circumstances, you need not fear that she has been molested," the doctor informed Gareth privately.

When Gareth escorted the doctor out, he realized he'd

quite forgotten the runners and their prisoners, who were still waiting for him outside.

"Angus, you cannot know what a service you have done for me," Gareth told the man, "both today and in Dublin when you found those records I needed." He gave both men a reward, but doubled the one to Angus. "You must let me know if you are ever in need of anything. I am in your debt," he said to the grateful man. "And as for these two"—he looked sternly at the prisoners—"I don't believe you are highwaymen, but I shall see that you both receive jail terms for this day's work."

The felons were so relieved to hear "jail" rather than what they feared, that they thanked him profusely as the Runners led them off.

He turned to the count, who had rejoined him, and remarked wryly, "You'd think I'd done them a favor. I hope they don't turn out to really be the 'gentlemen bandits.' "

The count looked uncomfortable. "St. John, I think perhaps I need to speak to you, inside."

Gareth stared at the man in amazement after the count explained the entire story of the "bandits."

"So Daucey and this Richard fellow were the highwaymen all along?"

"Daucey had no idea that Richard was actually robbing the people," Maurice explained.

"Lancaster agreed not to press charges when you returned the jewels?" The earl shook his head in disbelief. "I suppose I should be angry, but I am simply too relieved to have it all settled."

"But is it? Aren't you afraid of what that Summerwood woman and the others are liable to spread about?"

"Quite frankly, I don't think either Lady Summerwood or Lady Bessinger are going to let what's happened here become known. I told both their husbands that if any of this is revealed, I would file charges and have their wives sent to prison. They all know that I meant it. I shall not tolerate Jessica being harmed further by those—women."

"I feel sorry for Summerwood and that Bessinger fellow. They both seemed too decent to deserve such tyrants for wives."

"I expect both of their wives will toe the line after this. A man can only be pushed so far. Summerwood said he's giving Vivian this season to get Meredith settled and then he's moving them permanently to that Sethmore cottage we looked at this morning. He's long wanted to retire away from the London *ton,* but she wouldn't have it."

"Well I suppose that's something good out of all this," Maurice commented, "but how near here is that Sethmore place?"

"A good two hours, thank heavens. Edward will still be welcome in my home, but certainly not his wife or her daughter."

"Meredith and Catherine knew of the plan?"

"They both helped with it. They are the ones who insisted a carriage be taken to the dock that morning so Meredith could leave Jessica and Daucey stranded after pretending your nephew pushed her."

The count shook his head wearily. "I don't think I'll ever understand women."

"Me either," the earl agreed. "Which brings us to my own aunt and Jessica getting involved in all this 'bandit' mess in the first place!"

"I do hope you won't be too hard on Elizabeth," the count said, worried. "I fear I am as much to blame."

"Not at all. They apparently headed out with the express intention of finding a highwayman. It was really my own fault for not supervising them more closely. But I think I shall leave all further direction of my aunt to you hereafter.

I assume you do intend marrying her?" Gareth added dryly.

"Well, yes." Maurice grinned. "I didn't realize you knew. Of course, only with your approval."

"With my blessings! I do love Aunt Bet, but it shall doubtless be safer to have her and Jessica in separate households, or Lord knows what the two of them will contrive next. You will kindly take Romand there—" he gestured to the pirate's picture "—with you as well. I don't wish to risk my children falling under his influence, as your nephew seems to have."

The count laughed. "I shall be most honored, but isn't that going to leave a large bare spot above your mantel?"

Gareth smiled. "I expect to have a much more appealing painting there very soon."

Jessica finished as much as she could of the dinner Cook had sent to her room and moved the lap tray aside.

"You haven't eaten very much."

Jessica looked up in surprise to find Gareth entering the room. "I'm—still feeling a little queasy."

He moved the tray to a table. "The doctor expected you might for a while. Aunt Bet said she explained to you what happened."

"Yes. I—I can't believe Lady Summerwood and Meredith would do that. Why would they hate me so?"

Gareth sat on the side of the bed and took her hand. "Believe me, they do not hate you, Jessica. I doubt they even think of you at all. Their ilk can only think of themselves and their own gain. You are to put this whole episode out of your mind, my dear. They are not worth bothering yourself over."

"I have tried to stop thinking about it—but I can't. Sir, Aunt Bet said that you weren't upset at me, but if all of this is told around London, you would surely not want . . .' She stammered and looked away.

Gareth understood what she was trying to say and drew her gently into his arms. "Jessica—" he looked down at her seriously "—I think I have made certain none of this will get out, but if it should, it wouldn't change the fact that I'm going to marry you. Even had you really gone off with that young scalawag and compromised yourself, I would still marry you—though I might well have killed him."

Jessica gave a sigh of relief as she slipped her arms about him, resting her head on his chest. "I still find it hard to believe that you could love me. I'm not at all the type of woman an earl should marry," she said hesitantly.

He chuckled. "I'm afraid to ask exactly what type woman you feel an earl should marry. But Jessica, I love you. You are everything any man could want in a wife."

"And I love you too, so very much—" she smiled happily "—but I am still afraid—"

"Afraid?"

"—that I will never manage to be a very *proper* countess. You know how things just seem to happen around me."

"I know only too well." Gareth grinned. "But you are not to worry about that. If there is anything you need to learn to become proper, I will be quite pleased to instruct you." Gareth rose with a smile. "But for now, the doctor said you must rest."

"Oh, you're—leaving." At her tone he turned back.

"Is there something else?" he asked, concerned.

"Well, no. I had just—it's of no matter."

The earl came back and sat beside her again. "Jessica, if something else is bothering you, you can tell me. Darling, I want you to know you can talk to me about anything."

"It—uh, wasn't . . ." Jessica stammered, not looking at him.

"Jessica."

"I did not really need to speak about anything. I, well, it was just so very nice when you kissed me yesterday," she finally managed with a shy grin. "I was rather hoping you might do so again."

Oddly, it never even occurred to the very "proper lord" to think what an exceedingly, *im*proper thing that was for a young lady to ask.